DEMON SCROLL

DEMON HUNTER
BOOK 1

TIM NIEDERRITER

COPYRIGHT PAGE

You can get a free Demon Hunter story and regular insights from the author by signing up using this link.

https://BookHip.com/KQDXQJ

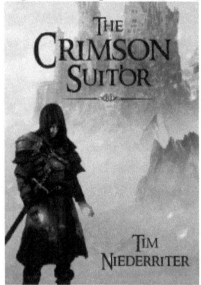

ACKNOWLEDGEMENTS

Thanks to everyone who supported me as I worked on my books. I owe you all a debt I cannot repay, but I'll still try.

Big thanks to the friends I've made through my online writing group: I Q Malcolm, Drue Bernardi, J R Murdock, Chris Winder, J R Handley, Kimiko Alexandre, and R Max Tillsley (Who helped format the first edition of this book for print). Truly, I can't thank everyone (Even those I didn't name) enough. That's right, even you, Nathan Pedde.

Special thanks to Reinhardt Suarez for helping me with developmental editing, and ebook formatting.

To all you writers out there, it's never too late to fix your mistakes.

Thank you.

Tim Niederriter, December 2019

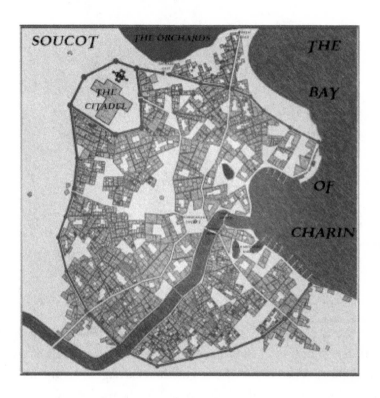

CHAPTER 1

On the last day of the journey south, the weather reflected Melissa's nervousness. Winds died away like the gale in her heart while a sweltering sun rose. She marched beside the wagons and carriages, setting the pace for the other guards on foot. Her fragile plains-hat formed a ring at the peak of her shadow.

The heat wore on the caravan as it approached the orchards near the city. The climate of the southern riverland left Melissa wistful for a cold breeze. At the edge of the trees, she got her wish. Cool wind swept in from the east, smelling of the salt sea and the coastal algae of the Bay of Charin.

Thank Mercy. Perhaps a blessing was upon her today. They would soon reach the city where she'd been born. Melissa once left Soucot as a child and not returned until today. She'd departed as an exile, though a willing one. Today, she returned as one of Lady Nasibron's personally selected guards.

Melissa completed her prayer of thanks for the breeze as a shout went up from the front of the caravan. Word quickly passed along the line from the leaders at the forefront, to the main body, and then to Melissa's unit in the middle of the long train, where the nobility traveled.

Her friend Orm, a veteran guard of her unit, brought the message to her. His dark brows gleamed with sweat under the broad brim of his hat, a grassland shade similar to the one Melissa wore. "We are to stop at the

Governor's Orchard," he said. "Tell the lady, if you may. I've learned she doesn't like men intruding on her."

Melissa nodded to Orm. "I'll take her the word."

He smiled. "I count on you too much lately."

"As long as you don't start to lean on me, big man."

His smile broadened. "Wouldn't dream of it. Thanks for jesting with my size and not my age."

"One must respect one's elders," said Melissa without cracking a smile. She turned toward the carriage where the lady and her niece rode.

Behind her, Orm chuckled.

Melissa smirked, but only when she was sure no one could see her. Seeming cold helped her avoid consideration as a woman in the caravan life. Melissa could be friends with Orm because he understood that fact. Most of the guards were young men, exactly who she would not want knowing she was anything but the best spear-fighter in the wagon train.

She found the lady's carriage. Melissa matched pace with the wheels, then knocked on the side-door. "Lady Nasibron, I have word from the head of the column."

The door opened a crack. "Well," said Lady Nasibron, an aging noble witch who sat on one side of the carriage's interior, "Out with it, girl."

"The caravan is stopping at the Governor's Orchard not far from here."

"We're close to Soucot," said Lady Nasibron. "Good. Good. I expect we'll meet with the governor presently, my dears." She directed the last sentence at the two younger women riding in the carriage with her.

"Of course, Lady Nasibron." The girl with Dominion-black hair inclined her head toward the witch opposite her. She made no motion or acknowledgment of Melissa at all. Melissa expected nothing more from any noble's daughter.

The other girl, one with nearly-white Palavian hair, folded her hands and then nodded to Melissa. "Thank you for the message." That was Lady Nasibron's sword servant, though Melissa did not remember the woman's name. She wore a dark cloak and carried a scabbard across her knees. A larger sword, the Nasibron family blade, was propped against the wall, almost as tall as its current wielder.

Melissa bowed her head, then retreated from the door and let the carriage pass. Her eyes followed the dark-wood conveyance and the four horses pulling it for a moment before she picked up the pace, hefting the spear strapped onto the travel-pack hanging from her shoulders. The cold wind escorted the caravan into the orchards around Soucot. She caught up with Orm.

"Did the witch snap at you?" he asked.

"Perhaps a little," said Melissa.

The plants on either side of the stone roadway were in bloom. Trees bore apples in all seasons in this place, kept by cycling gardeners who cultivated different breeds at different times of year. There was always fruit to harvest as a result. The book Melissa had been reading by the light of the campfires said the practice was centuries-old.

Her shift lasted through daylight and had been uneventful on the journey south. Most bandit groups wouldn't dare attack a caravan of their size, even if they didn't know a powerful witch and her sword servant were among the travelers.

If word of her traveling got around, Lady Nasibron's presence with them would likely be more a deterrent to raiders and brigands than any number of guards with spears and arrows. Melissa wondered if Orm had come to the same conclusion.

He breathed in deep, clearly savoring the southern air. His weathered face seemed younger, the lines less deep and pronounced now that they were truly in the region's grasp. Melissa was glad someone appreciated the warmth of this clime. After leaving Soucot, Melissa spent the rest of her young life up until recently forgetting the south.

The caravan came to a stop on the road beside the Governor's Orchard. Melissa's heart, for a moment rushed with excitement, even joy. She'd returned to the land of her birth. Those emotions quickly turned to dread as she thought of the possibility her parents might still live in Soucot. Melissa ought not to have to meet them again, given how they'd parted those nine years ago. Mother and father could forget her for all her concerns. She wished for a different life than the one they'd tried to push her toward.

Orm motioned to the bright, blue-painted roof of a pavilion down a stone walkway off the road. "That's the governor's shade if I'm not mistaken."

Melissa pointed with a finger as the shapes of people approached from the far side of the pavilion. A party of a dozen well-dressed members of the nobility surrounded a slim woman in a formal black gown.

"Governor Lokoth herself?" she asked.

Orm's eyebrows rose. "You may be right. See those two?" He indicated a pair of hulking men, both with skin a shade of light gray that blended to pale green. Shirtless, they flanked the woman in black, each carrying a heavy mace effortlessly, in one hand.

"I see them."

"They're demons," said Orm. "Members of the governor's forces."

"You're sure?"

Orm nodded. "I've seen men like that in the northlands too, in Wagewood, last I can recall."

Melissa had never seen a demon before. She frowned. "They look so human."

"Look closer. You'll see the demons' faces aren't like ours in shape, and they have ridges like horns over their brows."

Melissa squinted. "They're a hundred yards away," she said. "You have better eyes than mine, even at your age."

He shrugged. "I have to keep some kind of edge. Being sharp-eyed is practical, given our profession."

"I can't disagree."

Lady Nasibron's carriage rumbled to a stop near the path leading to the pavilion. The door opened, and the witch's sword servant descended the steps, using the hood of her cloak in place of a hat. She carried the small sword at her hip and the great sword on a sling over her shoulder in an ornate sheath and baldric.

After her, Lady Nasibron's niece, Elaine, climbed down. She wore a finely pleated skirt and a jacket of white over her maroon tunic. Elaine had spoken little to anyone outside the carriage throughout the weeks of travel. Melissa suspected Lady Nasibron would frown on her niece, a young noblewoman herself, consorting with the commoners.

When Lady Nasibron emerged from the carriage, she wore a dark hat and a smile that came with living every day for decades with a full belly. She joined her niece and her sword servant, then motioned to Melissa and Orm.

"You two, follow us. I won't let Governor Lokoth outnumber me by so much."

Orm glanced at Melissa, but she was already moving to join the three noblewomen. Any day she refused a simple request by someone so highborn was a day she risked her position. Orm followed her without further hesitation.

"You two are well on task," said Lady Nasibron. "Now stay at each flank. Aryal," she nodded to her sword servant. "Lead on."

Aryal threw back her hood, revealing long, bright hair. She marched up the path toward the pavilion. The other four followed her at Lady Nasibron's regal pace. No one rushed a lady with so much magical ability, evidently, not even an imperial governor of Jadiketz.

Under the shadow of the pavilion, dark-haired and dark-clad Governor Tandace Lokoth met them, leaving most of her party a few yards behind. She kept her demon bodyguards close. Did she fear the wizardess, or were the guards just part of the custom?

Melissa could not answer those questions, given her lower status. She'd studied many things in books, but the demons who served the governors throughout Tancuon were not among them.

"Lady Nasibron," said the governor in a smooth voice. "I've been eagerly awaiting your arrival."

"And grown older for it, I see," said the witch. "I take it you need me, or you would not have summoned me south by name."

"You think correctly," said the governor. "But before we discuss that matter, allow me to inform you of the other I requested who should be here shortly."

"You asked another wizard as well?" Lady Nasibron sniffed. "I'm insulted."

"Not just any wizard." Governor Lokoth smiled slightly. "I believe you're personally familiar with Deckard Hadrian."

Lady Nasibron stiffened visibly. "You'd summon that demon hunter here? At the same time as me? And you didn't think to mention that in your letter?"

"I hope there won't be a problem."

Nasibron snorted. "A problem? I daren't think you care about feelings, so in that case, nothing you would understand, Tandace."

Melissa's gaze followed the governor's expression as it changed from one of smug superiority, in knowledge and position both, to one of calculated coldness. That face Melissa knew all too well from looking into mirrors, from the polite smile to the chill in the eyes.

"You may tell me how you feel, Kellene," said the governor. "But in front of my people, you will call me by the title given to me by glorious Mother Mercy herself. You know what is appropriate. A learned wizardess such as you cannot claim ignorance."

"An impressive proclamation, governor. I meant only the offense you earned. Deckard Hadrian may be the greatest demon hunter who will ever live. Yet, he remains a man of questionable reputation. I will leave it at that."

Lokoth's lip twitched. Her face, still mostly free from aging lines in her forties, remained a mask of impassive and unemotional calm. Her eyes flicked to Elaine, where the dark-haired young woman stood at her aunt's side. "Girl, you are Palavian by descent, are you not?"

Elaine bowed her head. "As my mother before me, governor."

"Indeed. Your mother is an honorable lady, though I take it she does not practice magic as her sister here?"

"I fail to see the relevance of this, governor," said Lady Nasibron.

Melissa glanced at Elaine, whose face was reddening.

"Governor, my mother is having my aunt tutor me," said the girl.

"And your father? He is Palavian, is that not true?"

"Indeed, governor."

"Good," said Lokoth. "I take it you have studied the most common traits of the Palavian people, girl."

"Leave my student alone, governor," said Lady Nasibron, bristling visibly.

The demon guards stepped forward, each moving with precision, and no more than necessary. They made no gesture toward lifting their heavy steel maces. Aryal, the sword servant, tensed, stance going rigid. Melissa resisted the urge to reach for the spear hanging on her shoulder sling. Orm backed away a pace, clearly intimidated by the demons.

Governor Lokoth shrugged, raising both hands. "That's enough anger. I will honor your request this time, Lady Nasibron."

"Appreciated," said the old witch. "But I warn you. Don't push my student or me. Governor."

"Noted." Governor Lokoth sniffed the air. "I take it that goes for your guards too?"

"What would you have to say about my guards?" asked Lady Nasibron.

"Not much, I'm afraid," said the governor, smug smile once again curling her lips.

Orm made no response, eyes still on the demon guards. Melissa took a deep breath. *Too deep.*

"You," said the governor, pointing at her. "What is your name, guard?"

"I'm called Melissa."

"Your whole name," said the governor.

She bowed her head. "Melissa Dorian, governor."

Lokoth tapped her chin with a finger. "How long have you been in the employ of Lady Nasibron?"

"She's never employed me. I'm a member of the caravan guards she selected."

"Indeed?" Lokoth smiled, turning to Lady Nasibron. "You didn't even bring private troops?"

"I'm afraid not all of us have the same kind of resources as an imperial governor."

"It seems I was wrong to summon you from the Chos Valley. One mage, even one wizard, will not be enough to assist with my trouble."

"As you were equally vague in your letter, I must say, governor, this trouble of yours is still a mystery to me."

"And yet, here you are. The Magister's Guild will be displeased, but there is no helping that."

Melissa fought back a grimace. The mention of the guild stung, as the magisters had banished her from the south, those years ago.

Lady Nasibron laughed, not bothering to stifle or suppress the harsh sound. "I fear life in the valley is becoming boring, and for my student's health, I thought warmer weather would suit us both."

Lokoth's smile never dimmed. "On that, we can agree, Kellene."

"Tandace, it has been some time indeed." Lady Nasibron smiled, actually smiled, at the governor.

Melissa stared at the two women. Elaine's jaw went slack.

"Twenty-two years and perhaps a few days," said the governor. "When Mother Mercy chose me to govern."

"You made a terrible mage. The change has been for the best," said Lady Nasibron.

"I hope you're a better teacher now than you were then." Lokoth smiled. "Because I have a task for you along those lines."

"I already have a student."

"If I recall, you are more than capable of instructing multiple pupils at one time, Kellene. I wasn't your only student, last I saw you."

"I'm getting older, Tandace. And here you have summoned a mage with more experience than I if you need a tutor."

"Not a tutor. A drill instructor. And Hadrian refuses to fill that role if you must know."

Lady Nasibron sighed. "He still seems intent on taking his knowledge to the grave with him."

"I thought you hated the demon hunter?"

"Hate is too strong a word, but the man is bent on squandering what he has."

"Watch your words, Kellene," said Lokoth. "They say he can hear his name on the wind."

Lady Nasibron scoffed. "Nonsense. Such rumors mean nothing."

"I suppose you'd know better than I," said Lokoth. "can you train five mages in the arts at the same time?"

"I can, and have, trained more than that at once," said Lady Nasibron. "The question I think you should ask is how long such training will take."

"As quickly as you can," said the governor. "And as thoroughly."

"Tandace, you realize training quickly, and training thoroughly are opposed elements, like fire and water or sprites and banes."

"And yet, sprites and banes coexist in every mortal heart, balanced by the mind and spirit." Governor Lokoth smiled. "How long would you estimate before your students can be battle-ready?"

"Elaine," said Lady Nasibron. "How long have you been studying battle spells?"

"Two years, teacher."

"Are you ready for a battle, Elaine?"

"I'd ask not to be tested in one."

Lady Nasibron nodded. "And how long before you may study a sacra scroll?"

"Another year, at least," said Elaine.

"Correct. You see, governor, I agree with her. I won't push a student of mine into battle before he or she is prepared for it. To do so would be the utmost waste of time and energy."

"Is that so?" Lokoth shook her head. "What can you do in four months?"

"That depends on the students," said Lady Nasibron. "Those with clever minds and strong prior studies may pick up the skills fast enough to fight in that time."

Melissa's heartbeat grew louder in her ears. They were talking about training mages, maybe more than mages but wizards with the power to take on sacra forms. She stood still and attentive, enraptured by the conversation. To think, she'd been lucky enough to be called over by Nasibron out of sheer coincidence. Or was her placement another blessing from on high?

Clouds to the north parted, revealing the distant arc of the world's rings, the nearest of which gleamed brighter and a more metallic gold than the others. A warm draft rustled the clothes in the pavilion as the wind shifted.

"Perhaps we ought to search the skies," said the governor. "Hadrian may be due to arrive, given the way things are moving."

Lady Nasibron shrugged. "You remember some things from your studies, I see."

"You think too positively of my younger self," said Lokoth.

Lady Nasibron snorted in derision. "Obviously."

"Bring your people," said the governor. "Walk with me."

"You want to see him approach?"

"Of course. When I grew up, Hadrian's beauty and powers were legendary."

"Likewise," said Lady Nasibron.

The party followed the witch and the governor out of the pavilion into the hot light of day. Melissa and the others gazed at the bright heavens. Though they spoke of Deckard Hadrian, Melissa doubted she would see the immortal demon hunter in the sky.

In all of Jadiketz, only two men were said to live forever. Cyrus Bode of the Chos Valley, far to the north where the imperial capital once stood, was one of them. Deckard Hadrian was the other. In Melissa's books, she had read of others, but of the many who once claimed the gift of youth and life eternal, only two remained.

"There!" Orm pointed. "The lord of winds!"

The others, except for the impassive demon guards, crowded to him, following his gesture to the sky with their collective gaze. Melissa squinted against the light of the noonday sun. A gleaming speck of reflected light grew above them as the shape began to resolve. The form of a man grew clear as he approached. The man wore a robe of polished iron. The garment looked black against the sky but for glints of brighter metal on his shoulders and his wide belt.

How could he fly with such weight on his back and no wings? Melissa furrowed her brow. He was a mage, for certain, but she lacked the studies to say what one required to wield such an ability as flight.

As Hadrian drew closer, his long black hair flowed free behind him, rippling in the wind. He wore a sword at his side, sheathed in a black scabbard, and he carried a pack over one shoulder. At first, he seemed alone. Yet, as he reached the air over the pavilion, Elaine cried a warning and pointed to the sky above him.

A creature half-again Deckard's height dove toward him in near-freefall, leathery reptilian wings held close to a scaly humanoid body. The creature swooped toward the man in the iron robe.

"What is that?" asked Melissa.

"A vakari warrior." The governor's lips trembled. "Most likely that creature is trained in magic, as well. Get back, everyone."

The governor's party of hangers-on scrambled for the pavilion. Elaine and Aryal took Lady Nasibron and led her to the building, moving faster than Melissa guessed the aging witch could manage on her own.

Orm and Melissa brought up the rear with the two demon guards and the governor herself. Melissa hadn't gotten a positive first impression from Lokoth. Yet, the governor showed her nature in a crisis, springing to protect her citizens first.

The vakari warrior screeched an inhuman cry as Hadrian hurled it from the air. The reptilian creature struck the ground, not ten yards from where Melissa and Orm retreated beside the governor.

The lizard man roared, staggering upright. He loomed, over three yards tall, built thick in the upper body to support the pinions that until a moment ago held him aloft. Deckard Hadrian descended toward the aggressor, surrounded by the sound of unseen trumpets playing a divine symphony. The vakari warrior turned, eyes locking on the governor.

The reptile said no words, but the murderous intent evident in that gaze told Melissa everything she needed to know. The vakari wove a sign in the air, making a sound like chattering vermin. The demon guards lunged to fill the space between their mortal charge and the governor. Orm dove for cover behind one of the supports of the pavilion.

The song ringing from Deckard Hadrian grew louder as he raced toward the vakari. The creature beat his wings, hurling himself sideways on the breeze Hadrian rode toward it. The man in the iron robe hit the ground like a thunderclap where the dragon creature had stood. But the warrior already sailed overhead, flames dancing to discordant songs at the ends of his clawed hands.

"An attack spell," said the governor through clenched teeth.

Melissa stared as the vakari flew toward them, building the ball of fire in both hands.

Deckard turned and took to the air on another updraft that seemed to come from nowhere, but it pushed him in an arc away from the dragon man. He would be too late if the vakari hurled those flames. The reptilian warrior"s eyes narrowed as he probably realized the same thing as Melissa.

With a rasping laugh, the lizard man hurled his magical fire at the governor. Melissa shoved Governor Lokoth to one side. The blast struck her, carrying not just the heat of a flame, but a weight like a huge bludgeoning fist. The world shattered like a glass mirror around her, and she flew backward into a beam supporting one of the pavilion's arches. The wooden column splintered. She fell to the stone floor, black spots swimming in her vision. She fought to breathe, to return some air to her lungs. Her spear's head clacked against the tile.

Yet, everything seemed alright somehow. Melissa lay on her side, her world moving gently, in falling fragments.

In one fragment, the demon guards raced to the governor's side.

In a second shard of consciousness, one filled with the sound of blessed music, Deckard Hadrian seized the towering vakari warrior by the throat. He lifted the creature with him in one hand as he took to the air.

In the next falling mirror glimpse, Melissa saw the vakari warrior crashed down in a broken heap.

The shards of perception hit the ground and the fragments began to fit together.

Orm and Elaine rushed to Melissa's side. Aryal, her small sword drawn, advanced on the fallen vakari. Deckard Hadrian's face appeared before Melissa. Then the world went dark.

CHAPTER 2

MELISSA

The sound of rain on wooden rooftops woke her. Outside a high, arched window across the room from the unfamiliar bed where she lay, mist rose from an unseen river and obscured the shapes of buildings outside. She recognized Soucot, though this wasn't an angle she'd ever seen it from before.

She couldn't see the governor's palace anywhere. *Strange.* The damn building, as her father once called it, took up most of the hilltop citadel on its own. Thunder cracked the sky. Lightning flickered. Given that she could see anything out there in the little remaining light, she guessed it was still daytime.

Someone had bandaged her chest. She saw no sign of her tunic or pads of armor for her arms or shoulders. She suspected not much of the tunic would have survived that fire, though she still lived. Little pain lingered where the blast struck. Her shoes sat by the door of the stone chamber. Her trousers and breeches remained untouched, except for the loosening of the laces at the waist. Her belt was looped over a stool by the door. Melissa's spear and pack stood propped against the same seat, shoulder sling coiled on the top of the bag.

Funny how awakening in an unknown room could be soothing. Melissa moved her legs, noticing the smooth sheets were linen, so they must be expensive. Except for a light, vaguely pulsing, burn above the elbow on her left arm, she sensed no pain. Her senses were kinder than expected after watching the world fall apart around her.

She stretched her legs, then got to her feet. The air was cold, at least for the south. She brought the top of the linens with her, wrapped around her shoulders and chest like a mantle. On the far side of the room stood a cabinet with a mirror on the wall corner to it.

Melissa walked to the door leading out of the room and found it open. She turned the knob and peered around. No one waited in the elegantly-tiled hallway outside. She turned to see a tall man step off the windowsill and onto the floor near the bed. Traces of rain dripped onto the floor.

She grabbed her spear, letting the sheets cascade off her. An instant later, she recognized the iron robe and the gleaming iron robe, the ring of the belt, the long black hair.

"Deckard Hadrian," she said.

"Yes. And you won't need the spear. I'm not here to hurt you."

She relaxed her stance but kept her hold on the weapon. "Where are we?"

"This is the governor's palace in Soucot."

She snapped her fingers. "I should have known when I couldn't see it out the window."

"You know, you have a hint of the accent, but you don't look like a local girl."

"I was born in Soucot, but I've lived in the north."

"That doesn't explain my thought, but thank you."

"I think you should explain something to me...How did I get here? I remember the pavilion. The fire hit me, then nothing."

"Nothing after? That's too bad."

Melissa frowned. "What do you mean by that?"

"You talked from your unconsciousness. Don't worry, nothing abnormal."

"Do you listen to many unconscious people talk?"

"Over time, the incidents add up."

"How old are you, anyway?"

"As of this year, three hundred and forty-four years." He smiled slightly. "I've been on enough battlefields to know a serious injury when I see it. I flew you here within the hour, and the governor's physicians healed you. The process proved difficult, so they weren't sure if or when you'd awake."

"If?"

"I had every confidence you would survive. I will add, that most humans would be dead immediately given the power that vakari put behind his final spell."

She turned her gaze on her bandaged chest. "The pain when it hit me agrees with you. I can't say if either if that's correct, though."

Deckard's smile grew by a twitch of the lips. His pale green eyes gleamed.

"Do you think your feeling was wrong? I don't."

"Why do you say that?"

"Tell me. Did you hear anything during the fighting yesterday?"

"Yesterday? I've been asleep for a whole day?"

"Slightly more, according to the clocks across the bay in Kanor, I'd wager." He shrugged, then sat down on the windowsill.

Melissa set the spear beside the door frame. She approached the window cautiously. "You don't know why I survived."

"I've been trying to find out. Did you hear any sound, in particular from me or our reptilian attacker?"

She frowned in thought. "I did. When the assassin started making the spell, I almost thought rats were fighting in my ears. And you..." Heat rushed to her cheeks. "You made a sound like music, trumpets."

He nodded. "So, you can hear them."

"Hear who?"

"Call them essences. Call them sprites and banes, they're the particle entities of all magic. The ability to hear them is not uncommon. Most people can learn or hone the technique with the right teacher."

"I've never been taught any magic."

He slid to one side and patted the broad expanse of windowsill beside him. "Have a seat then, talented caravan guard."

Melissa rolled her eyes. She sat a few spans from him. "My name is Melissa."

Deckard nodded. Thunder rolled over the bay, echoing through the streets of Soucot and the arched window where the two of them sat. With Deckard silent, Melissa glanced at his face. "You say I'm talented. With magic?"

"Yes."

"Do you think I could become a mage? A real mage?"

"Most people have that ability. I suspect you already are a mage, just not a trained one."

"People can't be born as mages," she said. "I read that much."

"There, you read wrong, though such people are rare in Tancuon. However, I would also wager you were not born recently. Were you, Melissa?"

Her face grew hot. "I'm nineteen. You think I'm already a mage? Look, I was turned away from schooling when I was younger."

"Foolish teachers are beyond help," he said.

"It wasn't because I lacked talent, according to them."

Deckard gave her a gentle smile. "Perhaps you can tell me the rest of the story some other time. For now, the governor should know you are awake. I'm sure she'll want to grant you a reward in return for saving her life."

"I saved her?"

"You did." Deckard rose, then walked to the door. "I'll have Governor Lokoth send you a new tunic at the very least. Forgive my intrusion on your privacy."

"What about the rest of the caravan? My friend Orm?"

"You and our attacker were the only ones hurt in the fight. Your fellow guards are staying near here, beyond the citadel walls. I will send you their direction after you meet with the governor."

"Thank you," she said. "You did most of the saving."

"It's the nature of a storm to arrive with both thunder and lightning."

"What does that mean?"

"Every action has a reaction. Lightning is action. Thunder, reaction."

"And which are you?"

"Melissa, I'm a man. I only ride the winds." He slipped out the door without a sound.

Melissa shook her head, then turned to look out the window over the city. Her parents and her brother were probably out there somewhere. She sighed.

Not long after Deckard left the chamber, two of the governor's gentle servants arrived at her door. The man stood outside. The female servant entered and laid a beautiful tunic with laced patterns on its sleeves and waist on the bed.

Melissa tried it on. As she was taller than most women, it fit her shoulders and chest well but left her navel bare.

"I'm afraid for the sake of time, we only have one size," said the gentle maid.

"It's lovely. Thank you."

The woman smiled. "When you're ready, follow me to the court's hall."

"Of course. Let's go at once."

"As you wish." The gentle maid led the way into the hall. Melissa glanced at her spear. The gentleman noticed her looking and shook his head. "No weapons at court. You can come back for it later."

Melissa nodded. The woman led, and the man followed her down a flight of stairs, then around a corner to a pair of enormous double doors that they quickly passed through.

The governor's court surrounded them. Dozens of nobles, gathered in the wings, watched while Melissa and the gentle servants proceeded up a sea-green carpet toward the high seat. Before the throne stood a table, cut into two halves that arced in slender curves on either side of the carpet leading to the raised portion of the floor where the governor resided in authority.

The servants left Melissa's side. Nervous, she walked to the midpoint between the two tables, where in times of council, when all the authorities of Jadiketz would meet in one place, every governor and prince could be seated. She remembered the etiquette of a petitioner from one of her books. She sank to one knee at the center point of the carpet, head bowed.

"That is a polite gesture," said Governor Lokoth, voice echoing from her throne. Her words resonated, audible at full volume throughout the entire court, thanks to the room's design. "But unnecessary for someone who saved my esteemed life only yesterday. Rise, and remind me of your name, and who you are."

Melissa raised her head. She looked at the governor. "My name. Is Melissa Dorian. I am a caravan guard, born in Soucot. Only yesterday, I returned after nine years of traveling."

Governor Lokoth smiled, resting her head against the center of the sunrise pattern etched into her silver seat of office.

"Melissa Dorian of Soucot, I take it you have seen many things in your travels. I've witnessed many strange sights in my time, as well. Yet, my advisers and I cannot tell me how you lived through your heroic action. I mean no insult by the words I choose. How could a simple caravan guard, an ordinary woman, survive such a fiery blast as you prevented from striking me?"

"I confess, I do not know either, your serenity."

"You acted to save me without thought to your survival. You may have been born in my lands, but anyone who does such a bold service to this seat of Mercy and the person who sits it will be given a reward. I promise all of you. This is truth." She motioned to the assembled nobles and petitioners filling the rest of the room. "Tell me, Melissa Dorian, how can I repay your act of heroism?"

Melissa met the governor's gaze, fighting the urge of the bile rising in her stomach. "Please, your serenity, give me the honor to serve you as a battle mage. I will need training, but I've always wished to learn the ways of magic."

"Not money or holdings? You truly ask me for training?"

"In my travels, I've seen nothing to compare to what mages can do." She bit her lip and considered the way the Magister's Guild controlled the training of mages in Soucot and the whole of the southern region. The governor would refuse if she wanted to maintain respect for her alliance with the guild that had banned Melissa from practicing the craft.

"It shall be done," said the governor. "You will have every resource I can offer so long as you serve my seat of Mercy. With that, I will give you one more gift, though you may not yet understand why I offer it."

Melissa bowed low.

"I will let you choose again when you wish to leave my service. Until that day, I welcome you to my court, Melissa Dorian."

"Your serenity is generous."

"Am I not?" Governor Lokoth smiled.

The storm raged well until sunset. Melissa rested through the dark of day, for once, far from the dangers of the wilderness.

CHAPTER 3

SABEN

Night fell over the westernmost city in Kanor. Two travelers woke to descend to the darkening streets, heedless of the warnings spread by the native people. Saben and Jaswei needed the night to cross the bay. As he crept from their room, her footsteps were inaudible behind him.

Taking the charm that the man in the mask had traded them for their camel, Saben and Jaswei left the inn hours after sunset. The haunting ghosts of the wrecks in the bay were sure to rise if they existed. Having watched the masked man depart on camel-back for the south that afternoon, Saben saw no other choice than to use the charm. The masked man called the stone a nightcaller and said it contained a captive essence strong enough to help travelers cross the bay.

A nightcaller could perform its feat to summon a creature beyond the knowledge of the mortal world, but only by night. An odd hum of magic came from the glistening black stone but Saben didn't understand its tone fully. Summoning a spirit was a common act for mages throughout the world.

Saben preferred a blade to the tools of artifice.

Jaswei assured him she could hear the angry bane's discordant song, trapped within the stone. The glittering jewel offered only dull sounds to Saben's untalented ears, but he trusted Jaswei. As they made their way to the docks by the bay in deepening darkness, he hoped they wouldn't regret dealing with the man in the half-moon mask.

Saben had immediately liked the scholar from Tancuon but disliked the side of him that did. The part of Saben that appreciated an honest-to-darkness trickster was the part that endeared him to the man, no matter how fair the deal appeared.

He couldn't say he trusted the scholar. Especially, because with his bag over his shoulder alongside one of Jaswei's two large luggage cases, and his great sword in his baldric, he could grumble, but not much else. His voice would have to be enough to protect them if any ghosts attacked. The cursed sounds of his murmurs were enough to intimidate humans. A bellow could repulse or banish a haunting shade.

Jaswei glanced at him over her shoulder, the one not occupied by a heavy case. She wore the empty sword sheath she used to focus her magical banes. The sword that belonged in that sheath was long-gone, broken in a battle older than both of their years combined.

"We're nearly there," she said.

"Stay alert," he muttered.

"I always am."

She's too confident. Being the nervous one in any group never suited Saben. Tancuon was close. Possibly, he and Jaswei could part ways on the other side. He admonished himself privately for the thought, considering how little of the language she spoke from beyond the bay.

They reached the docks. Stone piling supported long and cracked wooden boards. A pale, creeping limb extended from the side of one boat. The haunt emerged from its hiding place, bearing the pallor of drowning and carrying the stench of death. Misshapen features were bloated from a life lost at sea.

Jaswei shook her head. "He couldn't have traded you a daycaller. It had to be a nightcaller."

"No use complaining now." Saben shrugged his burden onto the wooden boards at his feet. He unhooked his baldric, ready to hurl it aside and grab his sword at any moment. Jaswei set down her luggage case and then gripped the sheath at her belt with one hand.

"Let me see." She eyed the crawling corpse-being as it advanced on her. "Should I use one blade or two?"

"Take care," said Saben.

"I always—"

The haunted corpse leapt at Jaswei. Her hand moved to the sheath at her side. Sparks of light formed a singing sword in her hand.

She cleaved the haunt in two.

As the drowned spirit fell, it did not evaporate like the dusty bane-springing haunts of the desert, or the wood pulp of those from the vast jungle called the Bloom, but splashed into a pool of salt water.

"See?" Jaswei grinned, taking a guard position. She turned to face the other haunts creeping along the pier and over the decks of boats at anchor.

Saben drew his sword and gripped the hilt in both hands. His seal magic would do him little good against the dead spirits. In the gap between animals and demons, he lacked nonviolent magic for settling matters. He held his guard, not yet wanting to use his other magical technique, the one he held not in either palm like his control seals, but etched on his tongue in a faded sigil.

"Get to the end of this pier," he rumbled in a low voice. "Then, use the stone."

"My thoughts exactly." Jaswei leapt forward, cutting down another haunt with her magical blade. The haunts swarmed around her as she darted along the pier.

Saben followed at a meticulous pace, carving a path forward with every strike of his massive sword. The haunts showed no fear but disappeared into sprays of seawater when slashed. Living human bodies wouldn't last much longer against Saben's attacks, he knew from much experience. If only he had such success cutting down demons.

With a grimace and wrinkled brow, he hacked downward, slicing through two haunts at once. They burst into salt spray and then fell like tears upon the pier. He freed his blade from the wood. A broken board splashed into the shallows below. Skirting the new gap in the dock, he followed Jaswei.

She stood at the end of the pier, holding the nightcaller's dark shell in one hand and her ethereal-glowing mystic blade in the other. "It's not working."

"Can you hear the song?" he asked.

"Can you?"

"Barely could before."

"Well, neither can I now," said Jaswei.

The stone sat, dark and inert, in her palm.

The boards behind them skittered with movement. Dozens of haunts swarmed over the pier, blocking their path back to shore.

"That man in the mask cheated us!" Jaswei said. "I don't know how, but he fooled my hearing."

Saben gritted his teeth. "Stand back," he muttered, stepping between Jaswei and the horde of haunts.

"What are you going to do?"

He grunted in reply, then inhaled sharply. Saben bellowed. His voice roared across the dock, a wave of cursed sound directed in a blast of deafening force along the pier, just above the boards. Haunts exploded into a watery mist, then blew away on the echo. The boards of the dock trembled. Some of them broke into shards, splintering and falling into the quay.

Saben clenched his jaw shut as the aftershocks of his yell faded into silence. The pier shuddered as pilings shifted. More haunts rose from the water.

He inhaled again. Before he could give another shout, Jaswei touched his arm. He turned, letting his prepared roar loose in a low whistle. A shape floated at the end of the pier. Huge reptilian wings and a many-yards-long tail covered in sleek blue-black skin led to a humanoid body. Hair longer and even paler than Jaswei's streamed about his shoulders.

"You called?" asked the creature in the language of Kanor.

"We did," said Jaswei. "You're a fisher, aren't you?"

"My kind rules the Bay of Charin," said the creature, grinning. "Now give me that stone and, in trade, I will take you to the other side."

"What are you waiting for?" Saben muttered.

Jaswei climbed onto the creature's tail near where it joined the fisher's human part. Saben followed, gripping Jaswei's waist.

"Hang on tight," said the fisher.

Without waiting for a reply, the creature took to the air and flew toward Tancuon.

* * *

The fisher skimmed over the waves. Saben and Jaswei clung together, sprayed by droplets of seawater, and buffeted by storm winds.

"How did you reach us so quickly?" Jaswei asked the fisher in the Kanori tongue.

"We fishers prowl the waters of Charin." The fisher looked over his very human shoulder at Saben and Jaswei. "We listen for the songs of nightcallers while humans sleep."

Saben grunted, a low sound withholding his full voice. Even hours after their battle on the pier, he struggled to keep the magic under control when speaking. Jaswei held onto his arm with one hand, braced against the fisher's back with the other. The creature's serpentine coils danced over the water beneath them, far longer than Saben would have guessed from the stories of the creature's kind.

"You know," said Jaswei, "We're grateful you heard."

"I am happy to assist a fellow mortal. We are kin, after all," said the fisher.

"You believe in the common origin of our people?" Jaswei asked.

"Not believe," said the fisher. "But I can see it through the gaps when time's veil parts."

Saben shook his head, biting his tongue to keep from asking any kind of question, because of the risk it would pose. Jaswei patted his hand gently. She smiled through the dim moonlight of a clouded sky, gazing at the fisher.

"Thank you," she said.

The fisher gained altitude, wings catching an updraft. They flew free of the water. Saben felt a surge of gratitude for the smoother movement that followed their ascent. He gazed ahead of them.

"We're going to Tancuon," said Jaswei.

"What draws two people from the east there?" asked the fisher.

Jaswei glanced at Saben. He nodded. "My companion seeks to learn more powerful magic. Both of us have fought many battles in the east. In Naje, his deeds are already legend, and his name all-too-often cursed."

"Interesting," said the fisher. "And what names do you go by?"

"I'm Jaswei Da Enki," she said. "My companion goes by Saben Kadias."

"Kadias," said the fisher. "Like the suit of Tancuonese cards?"

Saben grunted in assent. The fisher laughed in the night as the moon passed behind clouds.

"You don't like speaking, do you?" the creature said.

"Saben's voice is strong," said Jaswei. "I'm sure you heard it."

"Is that what that was when I approached?" the fisher asked. "I understand now why he would be famous."

"He can speak, but the power is difficult to control," said Jaswei. "His legend is more based on his skill with a blade."

The myth of a man can weigh him down as sure as a massive frame and a heavy blade, Saben thought. He snorted in soft derision of the concept. He might have been famous in the south and the east, famous for his sword and his duels, but no one beyond Kanor knew him. *Thus ends my legend.* He smiled at the thought.

"You are mercenaries," said the fisher. "Is that it?"

"We were," said Jaswei. "We have not fought for coin in some time."

"They require many mercenaries in Tancuon. You will be well-suited to that place."

Jaswei arched an elegant brow. "Is that your opinion, helpful fisher?"

"We fishers see through time, but only one way. We know nothing of the future and little of daylight. The sun pains us, and always has."

"May the daylight never touch you," said Jaswei. "Though, it's a pity the night hides much of your fine shape from my eyes."

"Bless you, fair human," said the fisher. "By day, I sometimes take the form of a man. By night, wing and tail are my tools for plying the fisher's trade."

Jaswei smiled. "And may your prey never see your approach."

"You'd do well to remember these manners in Tancuon," said the fisher. "As would your friend. We will be there by morning."

"Good," said Saben softly. His voice emerged like a rumble of thunder, tinged with the hints of an oncoming storm.

The fisher glanced over his shoulder at them. "You can speak, indeed," he said. "I appreciate you wielding your terrible gift sparingly."

Saben nodded. He watched the water rush past below. The clouds parted, and the moon shimmered on the waves.

CHAPTER 4

SABEN

As the storm intensified around Soucot, the fisher left Saben and Jaswei on the shore outside the city. The two of them climbed off his back, and the fisher slithered to the edge of the water. The creature disappeared into the surf, while the light of the rising sun hid behind clouds.

Jaswei turned away from the roiling sea to look at him. "Now what?"

"We find a scroll, master its power, then go to the city." Saben stopped to blow warm air into his hands, dripping wet and shaking from the chill of sea spray. He cursed the storm silently.

"The city? It's over there." Jaswei pointed toward the walls of what had to be Soucot, visible over the beaches and treetops around it.

"You know what I mean," said Saben. "Not a human city." He waved at the sky. "The demon city on the ring high above."

"You aren't going to give that up, even after all this time?"

"I came here for my mission. Leaving Naje was necessary for all kinds of reasons, but I keep that one foremost in my mind." He began walking toward Soucot.

Jaswei followed, still carrying her half of the luggage with ease, despite the case being larger than her whole body. "Suppose you get there. Then what?"

"Then, I take revenge on the monsters that attacked my village." Saben's voice built in intensity and volume as he remembered his youth. He clenched his teeth to bite back the roiling discord with him.

"Look, I'm not saying you need to forgive them..."

He didn't look at her as they kept walking.

"...I just think you should keep your mind open to the possibility that when you get to the city, you won't want to destroy the demons. Who knows if the ones who attacked your village are even there?"

He shrugged his shoulders. "I'll think about it."

"You probably won't."

"Right."

They trudged through the rain, leaving the beach behind. Saben and Jaswei crossed a half-mile of open beach to the nearest trees, then went another quarter-mile to the walls themselves. The tall northern gates of Soucot loomed. Even in the rain, the sound of the Tancuonese language dominated his ears as he and Jaswei moved through the crowds of people. Locals and travelers alike came and went, walking or running over flat stones turned slick by the downpour.

They reached an inn just beyond the walls and got a table near the hearth to rest and dry. A meal cost them the last of their coin and trade of one of Jaswei's finer sets of clothes, kept perfectly dry from sea and storm in the magically sealed cases of her luggage.

With food, a smoky roast of local pork, and a roof over their heads, Saben took a moment to escape the misery of the last few hours. The last leg of their flight over the white-capped waves had been harrowing, cold, and wet.

A curse on that man in the moon mask for offering only that means to us, Saben thought.

The trek through the city left him hungry and tired. Yet, his journey continued. The ring of demons lay far away and high above the world he and all other mortals knew. He was done dreaming of revenge. Soon his goal would fall within his reach.

"What are you thinking about?" Jaswei asked, smiling.

"How far we've come. Where we can go."

Her smile slipped away. "The demon city? No need to worry about that. I mean, don't get ahead of yourself, Saben."

"I know. But in a city like this, I can find a scroll, the kind I need."

"Did you say something about a scroll, stranger?" A man leaned toward them from the next table over. He was heavyset and light-haired, with a wisp of beard about his mouth. A lute sat opposite him, propped in the chair, taking up space most often reserved for one's companion.

Saben tried his Tancuonese. "I did."

"You want a sacra scroll," said the man. "I'm a musician, not a mage, but I know where you can find that sort of thing, in exchange for a good turn."

"We don't have any money," said Saben.

"Lucky for you, my information isn't expensive."

"I'm not often that lucky." *More often, cursed.*

The man laughed and patted his round belly. "Fine. I happen to want something inside the library too."

Jaswei leaned forward, brows furrowed as she tried to follow their conversation. Even if this man tried to trick them, he didn't look like much of a fighter. Saben and Jaswei could handle a few local goons if it came to that.

"Where is the library?" he asked.

"My name is Rond. I'll take you there if you agree to help me get what I want from inside."

Saben nodded to the man. "I'll need to confer with my friend. She doesn't speak your tongue."

"Don't take too long. I won't be here forever."

"No one could be," said Saben under his breath. He turned to Jaswei and said in Najean. "How much did you get of that?"

"I think he wants to deal."

"He can show us to a library with an archive of magical scrolls."

"What does he want in exchange? I had trouble following that part."

"He wants us to take something from inside for him."

"Seems fair."

Saben turned to Rond. "Don't slow us down, friend."

"I won't." The fat man grinned through his whiskery beard.

* * *

The rain slackened off by the next morning. Saben, Jaswei, and Rond took up a vantage point atop a roof on the low hill overlooking the library of Soucot. Though it looked like a temple or a church with extra wings added on half-randomly, the building retained a bit of the grandeur of its original design.

Saben noted tall steeples on either end of the main structure, a wheel of towers sprouting from the far caps at the end of each additional archive, themselves large enough to dwarf many of the smaller houses around the building. Jaswei whistled.

"Big ugly building," she said in an accented attempt at Tancuonese.

Rond nodded. "The northeastern wing has the magic scrolls. That's where we want to go."

"Agreed," said Saben. "You know how to get inside?"

"Ordinary citizens are allowed in. I live in Lowenrane. Have all my life, no matter what I look like." He laughed.

Saben could tell he'd missed the minstrel's joke. "You don't look like a local?"

Rond shook his head. "You speak the language so well. I forgot you're a foreigner. Truth is, you look more local than I do with this Palavian hair." He tugged at the end of his thin yellow beard. "But in the land of mercy, all sorts get along, somehow."

"Is that so?" Saben folded his arms. "Answer. Who guards the library?"

"Mostly the city's archivist monks. Their cloisters are along the south-most wall of the city, so we won't have to worry about them if we move fast."

"Can you move fast?" asked Saben.

"As fast as you, I'd bet, my big friend."

"You'd better be right." *Curses walk the same roads as the overconfident.* Rond shrugged. "Oh, I am."

"The library is guarded by monks?" Jaswei asked.

"A few of them," said Rond. "There are also house guards from the governor's palace. They change them every few hours. Those are the ones who check you at the door."

"You can get us past them, I take it, Rond?" Saben said.

Rond nodded. "Between my papers and our appearances, we'll get inside. It's getting into the mage wing that'll be more difficult."

"Why is that?"

"The way I heard it, the governor has a demon guarding the entrance inside."

"A demon?" Saben's brow furrowed. "What kind of demon?"

"One of her personal soldiers. A warrior from on high, they say. Not like we see a lot of demons around these parts. We're too far south to worry like they do in my family's homeland. Not many wells around here. Truth is, you two look like you could take one of the governor's fellows."

"Do you know what it's called?" asked Saben. "This demon?"

"Not sure. All I know is the governor's guards come from the house of Mother Mercy herself."

Saben grunted. "That's a name only you Tancuonese use," he said. "If the guard is a lesser demon, I have a way to handle such creatures." He turned over his palm, revealing the demon seal tattooed on it. "One of them shouldn't trouble us."

* * *

As the sky cleared that afternoon, Saben and Jaswei left Rond to explore the city on their own. Saben didn't trust the minstrel. The Tancuonese people relied on demons too much, when no man or woman should consort so closely with the immortals of the higher world.

His father once told him something similar, though the exact words faded into the past with Saben's lost village and family. Saben's gut clenched at the thought of the burning trees. The thatch work of rooftops they'd spent the whole season repairing collapsed like kindling as demons bounded through the village.

Saben's old family name translated to Tancuonese as Thatcher. *A curse on all that straw and tar, long gone.* Even the deck of cards his sister and he played with until that day burned except for one. The flowering black ace of kadias remained, clutched in his hand while the others scattered outside his hiding place within the chimney of the house.

He once thought them safe from raiders, despite their nearness to a demon well beside a river in the nearby valley. Each child in his village trained to draw control seals and had one to stop demons tattooed on the hand. Those seals kept them safe just as those hands worked to build everything else they had in the quiet hills where the village stood.

Those hands, all traced with demon control seals throughout, had not been enough to stop the monstrous attack. When Saben emerged, every single villager lay dead or vanished as if into the air itself. Where people had fought back, they lay dead. The hands that bore their demon control seals were severed.

His sister. His parents. And Saben, though he was nearly a man at fourteen years old, clutched the card to his chest and cried.

That was when the white-robed demon standing in the town square nearby noticed him. He turned a blank gaze set in a smooth, eyeless face toward Saben. A thin mouth drew back. Above the demon's grin, the dome of his face became a void of reasonless, uncaring darkness lit as if by the twinkle of countless distant stars.

The demon smiled at the boy. Saben had no curses left for the monster back then.

As he walked through Soucot with Jaswei, Saben recalled the situation and imagined what he would say when he found that beast once more. He would lay every hex and verse of ill will he could upon the fiend who took everything from him.

With power in his hands and anger in his sword, he would impale the demon with all his might. He would lean close and whisper in the evil thing's abominable face. "Justice is mine."

At last, he would roar in a fury, as he once screamed in the ruined village, but finally, his voice would be strong enough to end that immortal life.

In the present, he moved through the city of Soucot. In the future, he would track demons through the streets of their city. He quietly vowed to take a scroll from the library the moment he could get inside. By the ghosts of memory, he wouldn't wait long. Laws of Tancuon be damned.

CHAPTER 5

ELAINE

Sometimes, when Lady Nasibron wanted Elaine to learn faster, she tapped her fingers to her cheek. Such moments seemed more and more frequent lately. Lady Nasibron tapped her cheek and frowned intently.

The two of them stood in the yard of Governor Lokoth's palace, their shoes growing wet in the grass, still vibrant green from the previous day's rain. Elaine wanted to learn as quickly as she could. She knew her studies were taking longer than those of most witches. For one, the pupils she'd begun studying alongside, under Lady Nasibron were all journeying witches or higher already. Some had even found households or courts to settle in.

Elaine took a deep breath and worked to balance her sprites, matching her hand to the clump of rock and dirt her teacher had given her to hold at the start of the lesson. Sweat beaded on Elaine's brow.

Lady Nasibron's fingers drummed against the side of her jaw. "You aren't changing."

"Not even a little?"

"There is no such thing as a little change in this case. Have you found your equilibrium, niece?"

"I'm trying. I have the image I need. I know it."

"Hold that image in your mind. Focus on it."

Elaine pictured the barren hill above the northern slope of the Chos Valley, overlooking the tangle of tree branches and mist. She imagined the castle where she had grown up, the home she'd not seen in almost two years. Elaine wished to return there soon. Her mother and father still lived in that place, and she wanted to see them again. They would welcome her in as their daughter, a true and honorable member of the family.

She imagined them as they had been when she last left them. Mother's hair had begun to turn from Palavian gold to silver. She wore a kind smile on her face. Father held his powerful arms crossed. He would be so pleased to know his daughter could fend for herself, at last. Elaine would be safe, and they would be secure in their later years.

She pushed the feeling of safety, of security, of purposeful balance from her heart to her hand. The stones remained, but the sprite song in her heart matched the low reverberations of the ground at her feet. Her body formed a bridge between the soil below and the stone in her hand. She opened her eyes to see the skin on her hand hardening as it took on the texture and properties of the stone.

Lady Nasibron's finger paused in mid-tap, hovering beside her face. "Maintain that." The hint of a smile crept into her voice. "Elaine, I daresay you're making progress."

Elaine gave her aunt a half-nod. She spread the form of earth from her hand to her arm to her body. She became like a living stone, balancing every sprite and bane in her being with the others over the next few minutes. She could still move, thanks to the effort she spent retaining her human shape down to the details. She opted to avoid any large gestures to maintain her mental focus. She stayed as a statue, waiting for Lady Nasibron to tell her what to do next.

Her teacher looked toward the sky. "That man," she said under her breath.

Elaine's stony brows bent slightly. *Could Lady Nasibron be looking for Deckard Hadrian?* She followed her aunt's eyes skyward while Elaine smoothed her expression. Her face would resemble a stone from the bottom of a river, the kind children picked up and marveled at while they were still wet, then left behind on the riverbank to dry and become dull. She focused her attention to maintain her mimicry of the rock. She was finally getting it, and inner security was the key, at least for matching with material such as this.

"You're doing well," said Lady Nasibron, nodding to her. "You'll be a witch yet, my patient student."

"Thank you," said Elaine.

Lady Nasibron turned to the sky. "Hmm...I think its best you return to ordinary," she said. "You ought to look your best when Hadrian arrives."

"Is he flying nearby?" asked Elaine.

"I could tell by the breeze," said her teacher. "When you get older, you may also learn to tell when the air is moving unnaturally."

"He can control the winds." Elaine carefully shifted her body from stone to flesh little by little, in reverse order to that which she'd first transformed. "But I've never known a wind strong enough to make a person fly that was also so quiet."

"You picked up on that, did you?" Lady Nasibron gave Elaine an approving nod. "Deckard Hadrian is called lord of winds, but that's not the only secret to how he flies. Any mage worth her salt could create the force to push something into the air for a moment or two. It's staying aloft most of us find difficult."

Elaine finished her reversal of the stone transformation. She set the rock she'd been holding on the grass in front of her. "He has a secret, then?"

"More than one, my dear. More than one."

"Do you know him well, Lady Nasibron?"

She shook her head. "We've met before. I would say I wished I knew Hadrian better, but that would be a lie. He's an intemperate soul, the kind it's best for you to keep away from, given his proclivities."

"Proclivities?"

"Mercy, Elaine, you are a woman now, even if you're still a student. The man has a way when talking to young people of our sex, so take care around him."

Elaine frowned. "He takes advantage of girls? That's awful, Lady Nasibron!"

"I didn't say that, Elaine. He carries sweet notes in his voice, usually when he has a bottle in his hand."

"A drinker too? Should you speak so about an immortal?"

"I'll speak however I want about anyone but Mother Mercy herself, Elaine."

"I'm surprised. That's all."

"Well, heed my advice. Hadrian has a pretty face and makes a strong ally. Just don't take one to mean anything for the other."

"Governor Lokoth seemed to think you knew more about Lord Hadrian than she did."

"I would say I do," said Lady Nasibron. "I've fought alongside him before."

"When?"

"Before you were born, I encountered him in the Chos Valley. We confronted a renegade wizard."

"I know you used to work with the demon hunters." Elaine took a step closer to Lady Nasibron's side. "You fought against other mages, too?"

"The things we don't know, girl...This only happened once. Parson Dane, the old bloodhound of Cyrus Bode, enlisted me to follow Hadrian's trail one summer."

"And Hadrian joined you?"

"Hardly, girl. But if you want the story, I suppose now is as good a time as any."

"Please tell me, auntie."

"I will if you can be patient, niece."

Elaine nodded, not wanting to put in another word, lest she annoy her aunt.

Lady Nasibron smirked. "We were hunting Hadrian, not trying to help him, my dear."

Elaine pursed her lips, fighting the urge to ask the obvious question.

"Not many people will tell you this outright. Bode and Hadrian, despite being brothers in blood and service, do not like to share each others' company, shall we say. Twenty years ago, Dane was always preoccupied with knowing where Hadrian would be and what he was doing. He and I and a few of Bode's clan knights rode toward the valley, trying to herd Deckard into a trap. Dane thought we had him cornered in a ravine near the southern side of the valley when we chased him into a cave. There's little wind in a cave, Elaine. He couldn't simply fly away."

Elaine nodded, feeling her brow crease.

Lady Nasibron shook her head, a smile playing on her lips. "We really should have known better. As sure as we chased Hadrian, he wasn't fleeing us. He was leading us. He had traced the renegade wizard Ugo Meere to the very cave where we thought we had him trapped. Hadrian moves quickly, so we followed him inside the moment we were sure he couldn't get past us to escape. When we entered the part of the cave Meere was using for his study, we found Hadrian fighting this rogue wizard."

"What happened then?"

Lady Nasibron shrugged her shoulders. "What do you think?" She laughed and raised a hand to stop Elaine's protests. "Hadrian shouted at Parson Dane that we were on the same side for the moment. Dane is a hound, but he has some sense of priority, so we both attacked Meere. Together, we managed to stop enough of his spells to give Hadrian a chance to get close."

"Did he kill Meere?"

"No. Once Hadrian grabbed him all the fight went out of the renegade. Not many men are as strong as the master demon hunter. Hadrian came with us to Empire afterward. Meere was hanged in the city a few weeks later after Cyrus Bode passed down the sentence. By then, Hadrian had flown free again. That was the last I saw him until he flew into the orchard. Now let us go. The wind is dying down."

* * *

Elaine made her way along the passage to the bell tower nearest the guest rooms. She wondered where Lord Hadrian had landed if he'd indeed flown to the palace earlier that day. Lady Nasibron said to be wary of him, but neither of them had seen the immortal. How bad could the man be with all the stories of heroism she'd heard of him? In the intervening two hours, she studied her texts and changed into finer clothes than her training tunic and trousers.

She now wore a gray-hemmed white skirt and a lacy green blouse. A light cotton mantle in the same colors as her skirt hung about her shoulders. No matter how she looked, she doubted she would find a suitor in Soucot. With her studies taking up the majority of her time, she would probably not be dressing for any court dances either. Elaine didn't precisely mind her near-exile to the south. Those dances had been far from her favorite part of growing up among the nobility.

Besides, a suitor or two wouldn't make her a full witch any faster. Bringing a husband to her parents' castle could wait until she secured her powers. Lady Nasibron frequently told her the most dangerous wizards were those only half-trained.

"They have all the power, but lack control," her aunt once added. "Better one should have no magic than be placed in a situation like that."

As a younger student, Elaine had watched Lady Nasibron deliver the children of fellow nobility a few times. While the process seemed simple enough, her aunt assured her it was not necessarily so. "Thank Mercy for easing this part of my work," she said. "Child-bearing is no easy task for any woman."

At the time, Elaine wanted to ask what her aunt knew about child-bearing, having never had a son or daughter herself. She bit her tongue. In the chilly passage of the palace of Soucot, Elaine remained satisfied by her intuitive wisdom. Lucky, because she had usually lacked such restraint when it came to her aunt. That moment taught her a valuable lesson when combined with all the times Lady Nasibron snapped at her for prying or asking impertinent questions.

Elaine reached the door to the bell tower where a gentle servant was sweeping the hall. The man wore the dark colors of his position with a silver broach on his collar. His skin was pale, and his scalp hairless. Lines of age marked his face along with a scar along one side of his jaw. Even the broom he carried in his off-hand looked hard-worn.

"Excuse me, gentle man," she said.

"Excuse me, Lady Tanlos."

"Please." Elaine motioned to the door of the bell tower. "Can you open this for me?"

"Of course I could, though I think if you try the door, my lady, you'll find it opens easily."

"I was told by one of your fellows the bell tower is locked when not in use."

"Indeed, it is. I had another request to open it, but a few moments ago."

"Who was it, if I may ask?"

"Why, the bold young caravan guard, I believe."

"I hope she does not mind if I join her."

"I can go with you to mediate if you wish, though I fear you would outmatch me in most altercations, my lady." He held up his right hand, which Elaine realized was in fact, a metal facsimile of the original extremity with locking iron fingers. "You see, much like the young caravan guard, I once made a sacrifice for my governor."

Elaine gave a solemn nod. "I appreciate your words, and you make a generous offer, and one I will take, gentle man." Elaine gave him a smile. "Thank you. What is your name?"

"Hilos of the Order of the Ford."

"The Order of the Ford? Sir, am I speaking with a knight?"

"Indeed," he said. "Though one long in the tooth and far from his armor. Please, follow me, Lady Tanlos."

He opened the bell tower door and led the way up the spiraling staircase beyond. Elaine followed. A question her aunt would call impertinent raced to her tongue. Before she could think it through, she spoke. "Why were you sweeping?"

"The floor gets dusty, my lady."

"But you're a knight."

"And the broom is my sword, these days." Hilos continued to climb, his tone cheerful despite any rudeness in her question. "I'm not the sort of knight to retire and rest my bones as if no deeds are left to be done. I'd rather make use of the body Mother Mercy gave me while I still have most of it."

"A finer answer than my question deserved," said Elaine.

"Curiosity is no offense when it is earned." He smiled over his shoulder as they approached a door to the tower's bell rooms. "Here we are." He opened the door and motioned her through while he held it.

On the other side, beyond the ropes and mechanisms and bulk of the differently-sized brass bells, the room appeared empty.

"That's strange," said Elaine.

"Perhaps not, my lady," said Hilos. "Our other guest may be taking in the view at the balcony."

"I suppose that's likely." Elaine picked her way to the path leading around the bells, then climbed the steps to the balcony on the second level of the bell room's wooden workings.

At the top of the stairs, she turned toward the view of the city below. Melissa Dorian sat cross-legged by the edge of the wooden floor with her back to the view of the city. Her wavy hair fluttered in the slight breeze. A book open lay before her. Elaine and Melissa must be of nearly the same age. Yet, Melissa somehow sat utterly still except for her eyes diligently moving down the page.

The former caravan guard turned toward Elaine and Hilos as they crested the stairs one after the other.

"Greetings once again, honored guest," said Hilos. "May I introduce, Lady Elaine Tanlos." He motioned to Elaine.

Elaine waved his gesturing hands away. "Please, gentle sir, I don't require a formal introduction."

"Neither do I," said Melissa, unsmiling.

Hilos bowed slightly to Elaine. She only imagined his back creaking with the motion. The sounds of the wind made any such subtle noises inaudible.

"Excuse me, but I appear to be the one who has worn out my welcome."

"You may go," said Elaine. "Thank you, Hilos."

"Of course, my lady." The retired knight turned and made his way down the stairs.

When he was gone, Melissa then turned and gazed at the city. "I'm surprised the old man made it up here."

"I'm glad to meet you, but must you be so abrasive?"

"Lady Tanlos, I hope you didn't make him climb those stairs on account of me."

"Lady Dorian."

"I'm not a lady," she said. "Call me by my name."

"Melissa, excuse me."

Melissa sighed, then waved Elaine closer. "No, forgive me. I'm on edge just being back in this city."

"You're from Soucot."

"Originally, yes."

"And you left for a reason. That's simple mathematics."

Melissa gazed at the rooftops around the river in the center of the city. Two bridges, both high and stone, but one far larger than the other, connected their respective thoroughfares to the other half of Soucot on the far side.

Melissa pointed at a building on the other side of the river. "You see that district, the one near the coastal wall and the southern docks? I was born there."

Elaine walked to her side and peered at the city. At such height, the smells and sounds were muted, leaving the grandeur of the architecture free to speak. The district by the south docks stood around the remains of a set of tall walls. Those walls were crumbling with time down to the demon stone that made up their black cores. Indestructible by mortal hands, demon stone retained its shape, impervious to the years. Such rock formed near-immortal fortifications. In places, though, the walls ended in jagged breaks, as if some force once hewed through the otherwise unbreakable stone.

Elaine frowned. "What happened to those walls?"

"They've looked like that my whole life," said Melissa.

"They're broken."

"Lots of walls in this city have seen better times."

"Please. You don't understand. The black shell of demon stone is thought to be impenetrable."

"Long before you or I, something did more than penetrate those walls, Lady Tanlos. It destroyed them."

"That is evident, yes. I wonder what could do that?"

Melissa shrugged. "I'm just glad it's in the past."

Elaine nodded. "You seem a practical woman, Melissa."

The former guard glanced at her. "Your point?"

"I'm curious. When presented with the opportunity of a reward, you chose the most difficult path I'd think possible, that of a mage."

Melissa turned to look over the city. "I know what I want, Lady Tanlos. I've dreamed of becoming a mage, yet haven't thought it possible in a long time. Now I have a chance."

"Thank you for your answer."

"Is studying magic that difficult, Lady Tanlos?"

"Some find it easier. I confess I am not a natural talent. You may learn faster than I have."

Melissa nodded. "Thank you for being honest."

"Likewise."

Melissa got to her feet. She picked up the book. "If you don't mind, I think I'll leave you with the view. I still have things to read before sundown."

"Of course. May Mercy follow you."

"And you, Lady Tanlos."

Melissa's footsteps sounded heavy on the boards as she descended the stairs, then left the bell tower. Elaine stood, gazing at the city, wondering about the woman and the ancient broken walls around her birthplace. Northerners were supposed to be of few words, especially Palavians, but Melissa Dorian put most of Elaine's people to shame.

CHAPTER 6

MELISSA

The inn where Orm was staying with a group of other caravan guards stood on one side of a low hill, south of the river. Dogs barked somewhere in the neighborhood nearby as Melissa drew close.

The place looked as run-down as anywhere Melissa had ever stayed during her travels. Yet, she couldn't feel too sorry for the guards quartered there. She preferred staying in buildings like this tavern, compared to the palace, if only because of the familiarity of slums. Governor Lokoth insisted on keeping her close for the moment.

"I like to have a hero at my side when I can," she'd said.

The governor's restrictions didn't change one fact. Melissa didn't adjust easily to the privileges and gifts she'd never imagined until five days ago. The myths of the mighty told common people their lives couldn't change. Without the influence of someone with as much power as a governor, Melissa generally agreed.

The wind and the dogs were howling as Melissa opened the door to the inn.

Orm sat at a table inside, surrounded by his fellow guards. He stood when he saw Melissa. She nodded in his direction, and he made his way around the table and then over to where she stood. He looked the same as ever, the same smile, the same shiny bald scalp. When he reached Melissa the light motivating Orm's expression faded. "There you are!"

"Sorry I couldn't get here sooner."

"Forget about that!" Orm laughed, his enthusiasm returning. "You're still alive, and it looks like you're moving up in the world. A lot of us here are envious. If you'd asked for gold or a knighthood, I'd understand that better."

Melissa nodded toward the table full of other caravan guards. "You can tell them I've dreamed of being a mage my whole life."

"Is that true?" Orm whistled.

"Close enough for them, I think," said Melissa. "Do you still have my books?"

"They're upstairs in the room I'm sharing," said Orm. "But come now, have a drink with us!"

"I never drank with these men before."

"Of course, but you don't have to worry about them anymore. You have the governor's eye now."

Melissa suppressed a laugh, her hand over her mouth. "I guess I do. And all it took was nearly dying."

"So that's how bad it was? I couldn't tell, exactly."

"Orm, you've seen people killed all sorts of ways. I couldn't have looked that different from one of them when the lizard man hit me."

"Oh, you didn't, but you seem fine now."

"The governor employs some excellent healers." Melissa turned to the table where Orm had been sitting. "I suppose a drink or two wouldn't hurt. But I need to leave before the sun sets, or people are going to ask questions."

Orm nodded. "Judging by the sun, I'd bet we have a few hours before last light."

"In that case, I'm buying," said Melissa, raising the bag clinking with silver from her first stipend. "Next round is on me!"

The half-dozen guards Orm had been sitting with turned in Melissa's direction, eyes growing wide.

"Not so loud, girl," said Orm. "I almost think you've been waiting to do something like this."

"Not waiting," said Melissa, finally smiling at the other guards. "More like imagining."

The innkeeper brought more wine and beer, and Melissa joined her first drinking session with her comrades. Because of her change in careers, she guessed it would also be her last. The drinks flowed with generous ease. By the time Melissa stumbled to her feet from the table, her vision was unsteady. She decided to leave the final bottle of wine to the others. Orm helped guide her toward the door.

"I'll be back for my books tomorrow," she said.

"Right, right." Orm pushed her playfully toward the exit. "Good luck with all the magic and reading, girl."

"Ha! You know, I like to study, but this was fun, too."

"Next time we're in Soucot, I'll get in touch," he said.

She steadied herself on the door frame. "Sounds like a good idea. I wish you safe roads tomorrow, old man."

"I'm not that old."

"Sure, you aren't, Orm. Don't forget to write."

"I'll write to you when I can!" He almost yelled over the laughter of the other guards behind them.

"No need to bellow." Melissa laughed as she reached for the door. The helpful innkeeper pushed the way open for her.

A tall shadow fell across her from the other side, cast by the setting sun's rays.

"G-guild master," The innkeeper's hands wrung his apron. "What brings you to my establishment?"

"I'm looking for the governor's new mage," said the obelisk of a man in the doorway. "Melissa Dorian is her name."

"You found me," Melissa said, looking up at the man's clean-shaven face, the same tawny shade as other local Lowenraners. He wore a gray robe, mostly hiding the shape of his body except for his height and thick paunch. A blue scarf of linen hung around his neck. "But who are you?"

"Such impudence. Don't you have ears?"

"Right, you're the guild master. Excuse me, sir."

"Oh, I'll do no such thing. Far from it."

"Guild master, she's drunk."

"No excuses will make the moon any brighter," said the guild master. "I don't think kindly of those who abuse their alcohol."

"Please, sir. Would you take this outside?"

"That, I understand." The guild master stepped out of the doorway and motioned Melissa through it.

"What kind of guild master are you?" She stepped forward. "I haven't been to Soucot in years."

Orm followed her outside but lingered a pace behind. One glance at her friend told Melissa she needed to sharpen up. The caravan guard's swaying image appeared apprehensive, tension lining his face.

The guild master chuckled. "I am the head of the Magister's Guild here in Soucot. My name is Ricklon Kadatz."

"Excuse me, Guild Master Kadatz, but that means you're a mage. I thought the governor was short on mages?" Melissa gazed at the man's face, where he looked down on her amid the growing shadows.

His lips tugged back in a smile. "You clearly don't understand. My guild is in charge of all magic in this city." He waved his hand. Two people, a young woman, and a nervous-looking boy detached themselves from the shadows. They wore the same kind of elegant robes as Kadatz, but of both of a darker shade of gray.

"Melissa Dorian, meet two of my guild members. I expect you recognize at least one of them?"

Melissa looked at the robed girl, a young blonde woman, probably at-least half Palavian, so a northern transplant or settler. The boy's hair was nearly as long and disorderly as Melissa's. The hair flowed to his neck, curling too much to tell its precise length, just like Melissa's. His face was pale and youthful, maybe sixteen or seventeen, like her younger brother would be now.

"Giles?"

He nodded but said nothing. Kadatz grinned. "You remember my guild now, I'm sure, Melissa Dorian." He motioned to Giles and the robed girl. "These two are my current favorite apprentices, Ferina Corem and, of course, Giles Dorian." His lips curled further in an expression of feral mirth. "Imagine my surprise when I heard your request to the governor. I had not known she planned to circumvent the guild's authority in this city."

Melissa blinked at him. "What do you mean?"

"Except for Mercy's temple, my guild trains controls all those who study magic in the south. Imagine my surprise that Governor Lokoth thought to build herself a force of warrior mages. I suspect she needs a lesson in who to trust with the secrets of our power. Perhaps it's fitting that you, of all people, be my example to her."

Orm squared his position at Melissa's side. "He means it. Melissa, what's the plan?"

She shook her dizzy head. "You make the plan. I won't be much help there."

Kadatz's lip twitched. He raised his hand, fingers forming a claw as he pointed his arm like a sword-point at Melissa's neck. "Because we are civilized in this city, I will only strip your powers, whatever they may be. You will live, but you will never work true magic again in your life."

"Orm, go inside," said Melissa. "No need for both of us to get hurt."

He glanced at her. She gave him the sternest look she could until Orm retreated inside. She turned her gaze on Kadatz. "What happened to the old guild master? Lord Jossetz?"

"Retired. Forcibly," said Kadatz. "You seem sharper than before. Do you catch my meaning?"

"I think so." Melissa turned to Giles, still skulking behind Kadatz to her left. "Brother, will you let him take my magic?"

Giles shuddered, fists clenched. "You shouldn't go against what the guild decreed back then. Melissa, you should never have come back."

She grimaced. "I see how it is. Coward, are you, brother?"

Kadatz stepped between Melissa and Giles, robe billowing around him. "You've said enough."

He drew his hand back, a fool of a fighter, telegraphing his attack so much. His hand formed a knife-like edge with fingers coming together as he stabbed at Melissa's chest. While a blow like that could hurt, it wouldn't do much damage on its own. The chattering sound rang from his fingertips gave Melissa's nerves a jolt.

She stumbled backward, narrowly dodging the strike. Her heel hit the base of the wall at her back, and Melissa's eyes fixed on the end of Kadatz's hand. "What's that sound?"

"You can hear it. Damn." Kadatz gritted his teeth, his mirth gone. "Ferina. Giles. Assist me."

"At once, guild master." The blonde woman spread the fingers on both hands so they flickered with lights from small fires.

Giles retreated further, as much a coward as ever. He faded into the growing shadows, then disappeared with impossible completeness.

Kadatz grunted and took on a defensive stance, too tight and too slow to be much use in most fights. Melissa still felt the impact of her drinking, though, and the mage's power could change everything. Ferina advanced to the guild master's side. Giles remained hidden by his magic.

The door of the inn beside Melissa flew open. Orm charged out, followed by a dozen other caravan guards. Kadatz whirled to face them just in time for Orm's fist to catch him in the jaw. The mage jerked back with a cry of pain. Ferina whirled, drew her fingers to her chest, and prepared to stream fire at the Orm and the others. She spoke a word of control before Melissa slammed into her from the side, sending her sprawling to the stones. Streaks of mystic fire flickered in the air.

Kadatz growled low in his throat. "How dare you? Common mercenaries?"

"Dare?" Orm shook his head. "Protecting each other is what we do. So take your students and leave."

"This isn't over," said Kadatz, backing toward Ferina.

"You'd better hope it is," said Melissa. "Because next time I won't be drunk."

Giles reappeared, his shadow cast a long way by the fading orange sunlight. He helped Ferina to her feet. The three guild mages retreated.

Orm turned to Melissa. "We'd better get you away from here."

One of the other guards nodded. "We'll go with you. Can't let those asses try anything on your way to the palace."

Melissa's cheeks flushed with embarrassment. "Thank you. All of you. I'd tell you not to worry, but I think I drank too much."

Orm and the others laughed and chattered as they escorted her to the palace through darkening streets.

At the gates, Orm clapped her on the shoulder. "Good luck, Melissa."

"Stay safe on the road," she said, then went through the doors into the palace.

* * *

Melissa climbed the stairs to where the governor had arranged her long-term quarters. The dark of nightfall crept through the halls, contested by small lanterns as gentle maids lit them and lifted them to hang on wall mounts. Walking with her head down, she passed a cluster of servants whispering among themselves as they worked.

"You almost look shaken," said the old knight called Hilos.

She glanced in his direction, not having spotted him when she entered the hallway. "I just drank a little with my friends."

Hilos smiled and nodded. "You certainly appear hale, if inebriated. Was there something else?"

She sighed. "The Magister's Guild came after me. My friends helped stop them."

"You don't sound scared."

"I had a feeling I'd have to deal with them. The guild is terrible."

"Do you have a history with them, Melissa?"

"I do. The guild banned me from studying magic when I was a girl."

Hilos nodded. "The governor will want to know that. Would you like me to tell her?"

Melissa shook her head. "I'll tell her myself."

"Don't wait." Hilos bowed low. "I must inform you that we are to meet with the other student-mages tomorrow."

"The others—Hilos, are you going to train as a mage?"

"I requested to observe the lessons. We will see if I learn something."

Melissa laughed. "I hope you do. I hope we both do."

"Agreed, Melissa." He directed her toward her chamber door. "Get some rest."

"Thank you, Hilos."

"Of course, honored guest."

She left his side and made her way down the hall. Once inside, she bolted the door behind her, then pulled the wooden shutters over the windows. The room went completely dark with even the starlight blocked from sight. She undressed, then felt her way to the bed and lay down to sleep.

CHAPTER 7

SABEN

He made his way toward the library, creeping along the rooftops while Jaswei kept watch at the street-level. Likely, she was distracted by some bright object or another strange sight of the city. Rond was playing for the coins of people passing through the square nearby. He, at least, was reliably absent. The man seemed nearly useless. Jaswei was competent enough for her flightiness to annoy Saben.

Neither of them knew, no neither of them understood, the vital nature of the scroll for his vengeance. His people could not rest easy until the demons that took their lives were finally destroyed. Tancuon was a land of demons and magic, no mistake. Saben would take the powers of this place as his own to wield for his vengeance.

Peering over the low buildings he scanned up and down the walls of the library's different wings. The additions to the building extended from the center like irregular spokes on a wheel. His nose filled with a putrid smell rising from the street. Distracted by the vile tang, he looked for the source of the stench below. Sure enough, he spotted a cart of fruit in an alley by a stand under the eaves of the building. Brown-spotted apples and mushy red berries wouldn't do much to attract customers.

A young boy who looked to be part-Kanori in heritage carried an armload of fruit around the corner from the alley to serve at the stand.

Wherever he touched a piece of fruit, its skin aged visibly, going from ripe to overripe and from overripe to rotten. The boy carried an imbalance of sprites and banes rarely seen in the native Tancuonese, according to Saben's reading during the journey west.

He snorted to try and clear the smell of rot from his nose. The boy raised his eyes and spotted Saben on the roof. He jumped, dropping one of the fruit he carried in surprise as his dark eyes widened.

Saben crouched and held a finger to his lips. The boy nodded, then started picking up the fallen apples from the stones. An old man, hair wispy and white, came out from under the fruit stands' sunshade.

He cursed at the boy in Tancuonese. "How stupid are you? Can't you keep a grip on anything you carry?"

"Forgive me, sir," said the boy. "I am both foolish and clumsy."

Saben slipped away from the edge of the rooftop to keep the old man from seeing him. Unlike the boy, he doubted the man would do anything to cover for his presence. Silently, Saben thanked his temporary accomplice. He glanced at the library as the old man stopped berating the boy. Saben sighed, stifling the sound to a low rumble.

"Look at what you made me say. Mother have mercy." The old man's voice carried to the rooftop. "But I suppose there is no point in admonishing you. Get that fruit to the front, such as it is, and I'll wait for nightfall to release you from my service. You'll get a full day's pay, in spite of yourself."

"Thank you, sir. Thank you."

"Your hands must be filthy, boy. You smudge my produce."

"I beg forgiveness."

"No more begging. Work!"

Saben crept to the other side of the rooftop. He waited in silence, just two streets from the towering library, muttering a blessing for the boy to keep his mouth shut. Only suspicious people lurked on rooftops. Saben didn't need any kind of attention from the city's guards or other authorities. The people here likely would not treat him well should he fall into trouble.

For now, the way looked clear. He descended from the roof quietly to join the others.

* * *

The doors of the library opened. Heavy creaking sounds accompanied the motion as Jaswei, Rond, and Saben entered the building.

Saben stepped into the library, finally tasting the smell of ink and old paper from the stacks. Rows of towering shelves ranked off into the depths of the great room from which the more specialized wings radiated. In Naje, he'd seen scriptures in their scroll cases, organized by their purpose and their laws of governance. In Crinri, he'd witnessed the opening of their metallic tomes of office with their appropriate majesty and grace.

Apparently, The Tancuonese did not value their written words so highly as those other cultures, despite seeming to have a great deal more of them. Jaswei's mouth hung open at the sight of so many books.

Rond nodded, a smile playing on his lips. "Stay quiet. It's the rule of this place."

Jaswei clamped her jaw shut, looking like she wanted to scream in joy if only to defy the rule. Saben understood the second urge well, though he rarely acted as impulsively as Jaswei. She grinned in silence and proceeded toward the stacks.

A small woman of middle-age with graying black hair and tawny skin, common among both Lowenraners and the Kanori across the bay, interposed herself between the three of them and the shelves upon shelves of books. She spread her arms to impede them. "Wait a moment, citizens. I am the librarian, and I would know your purpose here."

Jaswei started, scowled, then retreated a pace from the little woman. Saben stood impassive, grateful she didn't reach for the empty scabbard out of frustration.

Rond stepped forward. "I am a storyteller and performer. These are my assistants, here to help me compose a song about a mage of old."

"Indeed?" The librarian frowned up at Rond's bulky frame. "Which mage of old?"

Rond smiled. "Prince Geldingstar, who felled the demon of death."

The librarian's stern frown melted into a smile. "Well, of course, my friends. Anyone telling that tale ought to come here first." She motioned to the stacks on her left. "You'll find the histories and legends of Prince

Geldingstar beside the magic wing's entrance. Take what you will from this side of the doorway, but I must warn you, the one that guards the hall into the magic wing will not act with understanding to trespassers."

Rond bowed his head. "Thank you, my lady. We will heed your warning well." He turned pointedly toward Jaswei and Saben. "Won't we?"

Jaswei nodded.

"Of course," said Saben in a dry hiss.

"We'll take the utmost care," Rond said.

"See that you do," said the librarian. She stepped out of their way. "And if you have questions, don't hesitate to ask."

"We won't. Now come along, servants." Rond waved for Jaswei and Saben to follow him into the stacks.

MELISSA

Hilos knocked on her door to wake her before sunrise. Melissa met the others in the yard early. She first spotted Lady Nasibron and her niece, Elaine, standing in the palace's walled yard.

Near the witch and her student, milled some two-dozen other men and women, in clothes that ranged from that of commoners to the fencing gear sometimes worn by nobility, to chain and plate hauberks. *They must all be here to train as mages.* Given the governor's discussion with Lady Nasibron in the orchard, only four or five of them would be picked to receive the highest level of training.

Melissa joined the crowd, feeling under-prepared, having left her spear in her chambers. Many of the other potential mages carried weapons of their own, mostly long or short swords. One woman, a pale northerner by the look of her, carried two swords, one long weapon in a sheath at her right side, and the other, shorter blade, in a scabbard held in her off-hand. Some noble had sent their sword servant to train as a mage, it seemed. Her dark brown hair flowed about her shoulders, her black fencing jacket clean to the point of stiffness.

The sword servant spotted Melissa looking, then turned to approach. "Greetings," said the sword servant. "You're the former caravan guard, aren't you?"

Melissa's arms moved in an awkward shrug. "I take your meaning. Yes, I am."

The woman offered Melissa a hand to shake. "You have my thanks for protecting my master. I'm Suya Nattan, Governor Lokoth's sword servant."

Melissa clasped Suya's hand and bowed her head while the hey shook. "I would do the same again."

"I understand," said Suya. "That's why you're here, I suppose."

"Have no fear for your position. My ambition is as a mage, not a champion or bodyguard."

Suya smiled slightly. "I'm glad to hear that. Though, as a bodyguard, your heroics in the orchard were admirable. However, I fear we are now to compete. Only a handful of those present will be trained. Lady Nasibron is but a single teacher."

"I know how difficult the training could be." Melissa released Suya's hand.

The sword servant grabbed Melissa's wrist and held fast, keeping her close. "Be more honest. None of us here really know what it takes to train with magic."

Melissa frowned at Suya. "That's true. Now let me go."

Suya gently released Melissa's wrist. More hopefuls arrived as Suya apologized.

The crowd of aspirants now numbered between thirty and forty, including Hilos, the black-clad knight-turned-gentle servant. Lady Nasibron walked toward them, her gown swishing over the dust and grass of the yard.

Elaine hung back, watching her teacher and the aspirants with bright eyes. She could probably teach most of those gathered plenty about mage-craft herself. Yet, her naivete looked greater than her talent, given the expression of open awe on her face.

"Greetings, aspirants," said Lady Nasibron. "While I'm glad to see Governor Lokoth recruited so many potentials, I fear I cannot train all of you. For now, I've asked to take a few of you as wizard students. By no means does that mean I must take any of you. If your talents are weak or your minds unable to cope with the training, I'll gladly dispense with you all." She nodded as if to herself. "That said, if I choose to train you, I will require your utmost dedication to the art. All teaching is impossible without students who can reason and learn."

She motioned Elaine forward. "My niece has been studying under my tutelage for several years now. To be of use to Governor Lokoth, you will not have so long." She folded her hands. "The test ahead is vital. We will probe each of your spirit's to determine what power you bring with you." She turned to her student. "Elaine will test some of you to speed the process. Form two lines. Don't keep us waiting. Move yourselves."

Melissa joined a line leading to Elaine behind a young Lowenraner woman wearing a leather-armored skirt and a silken cuirass. The woman carried a short lance, sometimes called a dart, the kind often hurled by formations of soldiers before a charge, and wore a short sword at her belt. While they waited in the middle of the line, the woman looked uneasily at Melissa.

"I heard you carried a spear, Lady Dorian."

"I'm not a lady," said Melissa. "Though the other part is true. I didn't realize a weapon would be useful today."

"Always better to be on guard," said the woman.

"I agree." Melissa glanced at the other line, which moved as slowly as the one where they stood.

"My name is Niu," said the woman in front of her. "I joined the watch a year ago."

"The city watch, huh? Does the Magister's Guild ever run afoul of you?"

"Usually, they behave where we can see them," said Niu. "But the library is a center of contention recently."

"Is that so? Why?"

Niu raised her free hand and tipped it sideways. "I think they want greater access to the city's sacra scrolls. Their guild master is ambitious to train more wizards here than in Besany up the river from us."

Melissa frowned. "I notice the guild is still picky about who joins their ranks."

"They always will be, I think."

Melissa nodded. "They demand loyalty to them first. Never disobey was what they told me, growing up."

"They told you? The guild recruited you, once?"

"They did."

Niu's brows knit together. "What happened?"

"I disobeyed before I could begin training. The guild master may be new since then, but the guild hasn't forgotten."

Niu scowled, then quickly brightened. "You'll show them now, serving as a mage for the governor instead."

The line moved and the two of them approached Elaine. Niu turned as the aspirant ahead of her stepped forward. Elaine circled the nobleman, head inclined toward him, listening to a tune Melissa only caught in vague snatches over the breeze. She put a hand on each of the man's shoulders, gazed into his eyes before stepping back.

Elaine shook her head. "Best luck." She motioned the nobleman toward the other aspirants who had preceded him in line. Elaine beckoned the line.

Niu stepped forward and silently went through the same inspection as the man before her.

"Best luck," she said again.

Melissa went next.

When Elaine's hands clapped on Melissa's shoulders, a spark of electricity passed between them. Elaine didn't seem to notice the jolt, but Melissa winced.

The young witch narrowed her dark eyes. She matched Melissa's gaze. The two of them stood, locked together for an instant. A chill ran from Elaine's hands to Melissa's neck, then crept down her spine. Icy tendrils touched her heart, a feeling of utmost northern winter, colder than any wind ever felt in Lowenrane. Another spark jolted Melissa, making her stagger on her feet.

Elaine's eyes snapped shut. Her cold presence withdrew into her hands. She stepped back slowly, releasing Melissa's shoulders. Without a word, she pointed to the next aspirant in lone. Melissa frowned, then went to join the others who'd already been tested.

"That felt strange," she said to Niu.

"I nearly felt sick," said Niu. "And there was cold. Did you feel cold?"

"Yes," said Melissa. "It was like she reached into my chest and felt my heart."

"My grandmother says the spirit resides in the heart," said Niu.

Melissa nodded. "I understand that idea better now."

"Still, it seemed she reacted differently to you than to the rest of us." Niu tapped her chin with a finger. "I wonder if that bodes well or poorly for you."

"I don't know, either." Melissa remembered what Hadrian had told her about her inner sprites being unusual. "I suspect it may be a good thing."

"In the end, we never know what will be good and bad," said Niu. "That's more of my grandmother's wisdom."

"Your grandmother sounds wise, to be sure," said Melissa. "Have you seen Lord Hadrian around, Niu?"

"He left the city overnight." Niu shook her head. "I don't know if or when he'll return, but I saw him fly away last sunset."

Melissa's heart sank, excitement flagging. "Oh. I was hoping to speak to him."

"I thought you weren't a lady."

"I'm not, but it didn't seem to matter to him before."

Niu's eyes took on a distant gleam. "Lord Hadrian is quite a hero, isn't he?"

"He's a powerful mage," said Melissa. "That's why I want to talk to him."

Niu winked, then nodded. "Of course, Melissa. I'll take your meaning."

"I'm perfectly serious."

Niu smiled. "Fine, fine. Fair, fair."

Both lines ran out of aspirants. Lady Nasibron and Elaine met away from the cluster of aspirants, speaking softly to each other. After a few minutes of discussion, Lady Nasibron addressed the aspirants.

"Many of you have strong talent. For now, you are dismissed. Return tomorrow at noon, and I will have my decisions on which of you to train."

The clusters of aspirants broke apart. Melissa walked with Niu toward the gates leading to the streets of the citadel outside the palace. They talked a little more, then one of the other aspirants who Niu introduced as her brother, Tal, joined them. The three went into the city to find food for lunch.

SABEN

The more time he spent inside, the more the library made Saben think it was a prison for books rather than a place to honor knowledge. After four hours of fruitless searching, he returned to the others, hungry, frustrated, and sweating from the unnatural chill that crept from the passage to the magic wing.

"It is all in there," he said, motioning to the forbidden passageway.

"Best not to be fools in broad daylight," said Jaswei, trying her Tancuonese.

Rond nodded, jowls shaking. He smiled. "Right. And may I add, your accent makes words quite pretty."

Jaswei raised an eyebrow. She'd understood Rond easily enough.

Saben rolled his eyes. "We're going. This isn't finished, but it won't be done today."

"Agreed," said Rond.

Jaswei and Saben both glanced at him. Tancuonese presumption ran deep in the troubadour. Saben led the way out.

CHAPTER 8

DECKARD

Departing from Soucot on the western shore of Charin, Deckard Hadrian let the wind carry him northeast. He flew high above the sea, angling toward where the mires of Linien drained at the delta of the River Hirena. Stories said the ancient Hervs named the river Ophidia's Tail when they still walked the world. Deckard was not old enough to recall the time of the ancients before demons and maladrites contested control over the world. He'd read and listened to tales of old, sometimes from those who still lived from that time. Many of those tales remained unspoken for a hundred years or more in Tancuon. Yes, being an immortal in Mother Mercy's service carried its benefits.

Descending rapidly, he spied the river's mouth, rising from the morning mist. He must have been flying all night, yet the sunrise gave him only light. Part of his gift, one he rarely emphasized to others, was his lack of need to sleep as mortals did. A unique blessing, to be sure. Well, almost unique, but that didn't bear thinking on at the moment.

Focusing to stay alert, Deckard scanned the ground as he descended. The river basin was home to countless creatures, many of whom were unknown in the lands of mercy, west of Linien. Indeed, the river serpents were as powerful as many demons, though thankfully never numerous and slow to breed. Like many creatures left behind from the times of old, stories told of their shaping. In the lands of mercy, no one would tell who could create new lifeforms by combining humans and beasts. *No, to find those stories, one must look to the east.*

Vakari fisherfolk, wingless reptilians for the most part harmless to Deckard, came and went on their rafts as he glided upstream. He flew several hundred handspans over the River Hirena. His path skirted treetops that were home to more of the basin's plentiful wildlife. For all he could see, the place might be green to the surface of the swamps. Experience spoke to him of brackish fens and the dark trunks of creeping trees. Foliage obscured the shadow side of Linien from above, and Deckard saw no need to approach any closer. The wind carried him steadily.

He passed north of the delta, quickening his pace with a wind at his back. Cloying smoke, smelling of cookfires rose from either bank. Deckard ignored the native folk's mealtime. It must be noon by now, judging from the elevation of the sun. On the horizon, countless sparkling turrets gleamed like diamonds along the distant maladrite ring, high above the clouds, encircling the world. In times past, he would often fly to that city where Mother Mercy dwelt in all her splendor, though there had always been faster ways to reach those dizzying heights for those with magical skill.

Below, he spied the peaked dome of the Great Temple of Nassio. Constructed by the vakari nation that named it, the temple could have belonged in the bright city on high, not Linien's swamp. Brilliant reliefs covered in the sheen of gold-leaf glimmered on the walls. He circled the temple.

Marble passages lined with bone-white stone columns glowed with inner fire visible even by daylight. Multiple passages led into the temple on every level of the towering edifice. The dark shapes of winged vakari warriors circled the temple on patrol. No doubt, they'd already noticed Deckard thanks to his essence song and movement on the wind.

Once named as a foe by their master, he might become a target as much as Governor Tandace Lokoth back in Soucot. Mercy's spies had difficulty reaching the center of Nassio, primarily because of the difference in species. Among the creatures banned from dwelling in the lands of mercy, the vakari ranked as one of the most numerous and powerful. Warped by the ancients, they could prove a dangerous foe. Their nations often interdicted conflict between Mother Mercy's subjects in the west and the people of the Kism in the east. That last blessing, though unintentional, allowed many lives to flourish and also meant Deckard would be unwelcome in the temple.

He shifted his weight slightly from the sprites that bore him lighter than a puff of feathers, adding momentum. Pushing an updraft, he flew toward the highest aperture of the temple. A slender, balcony with no guard rail, wrapped around the dome, patterned with bright blue and red tiles.

Two vakari warriors broke from patrol to pursue him. Neither made a sign or sound of magic. With his lead, they could not catch him with mundane wings or weapons. He landed on the balcony, still light on his feet, then darted on foot through the passage into the temple itself. Some mortals and even some demons might call him daring, but in the service of his oath, he only counted such actions as part of his trade.

Besides, he neither heard nor saw any real evidence of magic-wielders within the temple. The looming stone columns along either side of the passage reverberated with the song of countless essences. Both sprites, and banes inhabited each column of white stone.

Deckard didn't worry about a foe-mage approaching using the column's song as cover. The vakari made powerful and unsubtle mages. If one of them wielded enough power to threaten him, he would certainly hear that individual's essences over the sound of the columns.

He stepped out of the passage, ignoring the far-off sound of commotion from the warriors landing on the balcony outside. They spoke in one of the many languages of Nassio the vakari learned with ease at a young age. This was the speech of their nobility. Deckard never spent much time studying the reptilian tongues. Even so, he was familiar enough with the language of the ring city on which the languages were based to understand the two warriors were requesting help. Caution served them well, probably saving the two soldier's lives for another day. Deckard glided to the bottom of the dome.

He landed not before the Lonely Altar, which he'd expected, but also before an ornate gold and essence-stone throne sitting in the altar's place.

Deckard's eyes moved from the high back of the gaudy metallic chair to the reptile sitting on it.

This creature resembled the warriors above, belonging to the same caste of lizardfolk. He wore a purple sash and pale, baggy trousers most ordinary vakari eschewed in favor of lighter wear. His scales looked loose, despite their polished sheen, the skin sagging underneath. The old warrior's wings were bent inward, scarred in places. One of those wings bore a particularly long, pallid, and puckered wound, long-since healed.

Deckard smiled at the sight of the familiar reptile. "I take it you've made yourself a king, Zalklith."

Zalklith's mouth curved in an approximation of a human's smirk. "Deckard Hadrian, healer, and killer. What brings you to my temple, old friend?" He spoke in the language of mercy, as Deckard had, though accented and tinged with the hiss of his people.

"Unfortunately, I think you already know."

"Unlike you, I've grown old since we last met. My memory is not what it was when you healed my wings. Enlighten me as to your purpose here."

"Allow me to congratulate you first. An outcast with broken wings must have a story to sit in a throne in a place so blessed."

"True, but I'd rather not relive or retell it, immortal," Zalklith's voice came out as a rasp. "I indeed have you to thank for this position, in part."

"I wouldn't diminish your accomplishment, old friend."

"Of course, what need has one such as you for a place like this. No human could ever rule Nassio."

"Indeed, not."

"Now, you know I do not see you as a threat. I do wonder why you are here. Linien is not kind to your race, Deckard."

"Lucky for your guards, I am swifter than they."

"Don't underestimate them. I expect they'll be here in moments."

"Quite so. They're probably still gathering strength."

"I told them to beware of flying humans."

"Wise. I only wish the assassin who attempted to kill the Governor of Lowenrane several days past had been warned of such. I would not have been forced to take his life."

"Oh?" Zalklith's facsimile of a smile slipped away. "Are you accusing me of foul play, Hadrian?"

"Do you know a vakari warrior trained in magic, with a grudge against the lands of mercy?"

"Of course, though not one. Many. Remember when Kanor fought Lowenrane? We fought both sides."

"The Lowenraners and Kanori suffered worse than any vakari."

"You know they did. You were there."

"And you? I don't recall you going to sea in those years."

"It was a different time. I was still clawing my way toward where I sit now." Zalklith emitted a low hiss. "Do not question my honesty, Hadrian. I owe you, but such debts only carry a fraction of the burden."

Deckard motioned to the altar beside the throne, a simple bone and iron design that had stood in the room for well over a century but never gathered dust. "I'd think you'd have gotten rid of this thing, after all the trouble it gave you."

"You were not the only source of my salvation, Deckard Hadrian. The Lonely Altar played a part."

"Have you become a true believer, then?"

"I trust my benefactors, though the more recent ones I trust better. Do you understand?"

"I see. You've made a deal with someone in the city."

"Quite astute as expected for an immortal man." Zalklith smiled, eyes cold. "You are not familiar with my newer allies. You can guess they are as welcome in the lands of mercy as I am."

"Are they maladrites?" asked Deckard. "Or renegade demons?"

Zalklith shrugged with one leathery arm. "My great high priest does not call himself either. Now, enough catching up Deckard. You've spoken to the purpose of your presence, so I hope your curiosity is sated."

"Sadly, Zalklith, you have only raised my suspicions further." Deckard folded his arms. The hem of his iron robe swished about his feet.

"We must all keep some secrets, even from our friends."

"I don't doubt that's how you feel. But I am not allowed that luxury."

"Such nonsense! How many times did you tell me the female traveling with you when we first met should be spared the truth?"

Deckard grimaced. "I lie at times. In other moments I may mislead. Such actions are necessary to perform the tasks set before me."

"Set before you, indeed, by golden Mother Mercy herself. Hadrian, you do not know what is right. Don't pretend you have authority to question my motives."

"I don't pretend, Zalklith." All ten of Deckard's fingers twitched. He eased the sprite strings from the tip of each digit. Every one carried a string he could shoot several yards on command. When tipped with bane darts, such attacks could pierce flesh and bone.

Zalkith's reptilian eyes narrowed. "Guards! The time is upon us. Remove this human."

Deckard hurled himself backward and upward, drifting over the white marble and gold-leaf plates of the sanctuary floor. A rain of spears pursued him, striking and glancing off the tiles at his front. He held the iron robe tight, knowing it could absorb the worst strikes of the vakari's weapons. "King of Nassio, I will take this as confirmation of your intentions."

"Do what you will, Hadrian. Let me see if you bleed like mortals of every race." Zalklith stood, unfastened his sash, and let it flutter to the floor between the throne and the altar. He started to sign a spell in the air before him, to Deckard's surprise. When last he'd seen Zalklith, the vakari lacked any magic training.

"Until we meet again," Deckard murmured, and leapt for the balcony above. At his reduced weight, his muscles easily carried him to the roof's apex. On his way down, he spread the robe and glided down the passage. He kicked up a breeze at his back and sailed from the temple into the air.

He climbed for the clouds, quickly leaving any pursuing warriors in the distance. Cold and wet, he emerged above a layer of fluffy condensation. Using the ring city and the sun to guide him, Deckard turned to the southeast.

The next morning, Deckard arrived at the southernmost port city of Kanor. The moment he touched the ground, he went looking for an answer to the larger question Zalklith had raised in his mind.

Which patron helped the scarred vakari take his throne?

CHAPTER 9

MELISSA

She arrived at the palace yard the next day, alongside Hilos. On a wooden board, suspended by a nail, hung a sheet of paper with not six or seven, but many names listed upon it. As they drew closer, Niu and Tal, joined them.

He squinted over the heads of the other aspirants, then shook his head. "I can't read it from here."

"There are forty-four names," said the voice of Aryal Hekatze from behind them.

Melissa turned to see Lady Nasibron's sword servant standing beside Elaine. Aryal wore fencing clothes, long hair tied behind her head, and carried both her sword and Lady Nasibron's great blade, in a belt sheath and on a side-sling baldric, respectively. Elaine's dark hair had been fashioned into a dozen black braids, contrasting with her pale gray gown.

"You're early," said Elaine. "My teacher won't be here for another quarter-hour."

"We're eager, of course, Lady Tanlos," said Hilos, smiling.

"But forty-four?" said Melissa. "That must be nearly everyone who was here yesterday."

"Indeed," said Aryal. "That's the record Lady Nasibron asked me to pen for your previous meeting."

Niu heaved a sigh. "I thought it would list those who were accepted."

Aryal laughed. "You should be so lucky. I think Governor Lokoth would wish the same."

Melissa frowned. "Is the governor that desperate for mages to help against the Magister's Guild?"

"Perhaps she is," said Aryal. "I don't know."

Elaine stepped forward. "For certain, we should not gossip about this any further."

"As you wish, Lady Tanlos." Aryal bowed to the young witch.

Hilos lowered his head as well. "Very wise, my lady."

Elaine's cheeks turned pink at the compliment. She coughed into her fist. "Now then, Melissa, may I ask you something?"

"I can hardly refuse, given your status."

"I thought it best to be polite."

Melissa nodded to Elaine. "Ask your question."

"Of course. Melissa, I heard you encountered the magister's guild master, Ricklon Kadatz. Is it true he threatened to take your magic from you?"

"I was a little drunk, but I remember clearly. That was his threat."

Elaine's expression darkened in a scowl. "I informed her this time, but you must tell my aunt if any guild mage threatens you again. They are rivals to all the aspirants here."

Melissa remembered her cowardly brother. Giles hadn't been her rival when they were young, but she saw the truth in Elaine's words. "I take it you're concerned for our safety. I appreciate that, Lady Tanlos."

Elaine sighed. "Not just your safety, but my own and my aunt's as well. I fear the tactics the guild may use if they sense opposition to their dominance in the city. At one time—"

"—No magic was done in Soucot without them," said Melissa, "I know the saying. I grew up here, remember."

Niu scowled. "I'd like to see those fools try to threaten my brother or me." She hefted an imaginary throwing dart. "They wouldn't have long to regret that mistake."

Tal nodded. Elaine frowned, looking like she wanted to correct Niu for her implied threat, as a good witch would.

Melissa put her hands on her hips. "Hopefully, we'll have better ways than weapons to handle them if that happens."

Aryal smiled, hand on the hilt of her sword. "Don't belittle the use of weapons, but I see your point." The sword servant noticed motion on the far side of the yard, then snapped into a formal stance.

Lady Nasibron approached from the far side of the yard, accompanied by the black-clad form of Governor Lokoth. Suya Nattan walked at the governor's other side, carrying both her's and her master's swords in sheathes at opposite sides of her belt. She quickened her pace and then pivoted to face the two noblewomen.

The other aspirants gathered around Suya to meet the governor and the witch. Melissa waited at the back of the crowd with Niu, Tal, and Hilos. Aryal and Elaine went to join the governor and Lady Nasibron in front. The governor held up her hands to silence the murmurs passing among some of the aspirants. Melissa waited, breath frozen in the quiet that followed.

"You forty-four aspirants arrived here yesterday, and I see you've all returned," said the governor. "Lady Nasibron and Lady Tanlos have informed me they tested each of your spirits." She beamed. "I wish to welcome each of you to my service today."

Niu and Tal exchanged glances with Melissa between them. Hilos' eyebrows rose. Melissa stared at the governor, unsure of what to make of the announcement. On the one hand, it boded well for her chance at training if they were all accepted. On the other, Lady Nasibron surely could not mean to train nearly ten times as many as the governor initially suggested.

"Lady Nasibron," the governor motioned to the witch. "Please inform them."

Lady Nasibron bowed toward the governor for a long moment. She raised her head and turned to the aspirants. "Training as a wizard is among the most difficult paths to the craft of magic. Each of you has the potential to achieve that kind of ability, but the key component is time. In the next four months, five of you will study directly under me, but the rest will be tutored by Lady Hekatze and Lady Tanlos. Neither of them is as studied as I, but trust them. They can teach you everything they need to act as henge mages, learning abilities to enhance your skills in combat."

"If you accept those terms," said the governor, spreading her arms, "I would offer each of you a commission in my service, as mage guards of Lowenrane."

Melissa stared at her, hoping Lokoth would not forget her promise or retreat from what that promise meant to Melissa. Magic short of wizardry could be powerful, from what Melissa understood, but the real power of magic was her ambition. She would not settle for less than the secrets the Magister's Guild tried to deny her.

"Step forward as one of my new pupils when I call your name," said Lady Nasibron.

Melissa locked eyes with the governor. Lokoth's eyes were impassive, her face stern.

"Suya Nattan," said the witch.

Don't betray my trust and offer mastery to your champion.

"Niu No Kaewoo."

Niu stepped forward, a smile spreading on her face.

Maybe I am too strange to teach the greater ways.

"Sir Hilos of the Ford."

If an old knight can be chosen...

"Kelt Crayta."

Only one left. Melissa's eyes narrowed. *This or second place.*

"Melissa Dorian," said Lady Nasibron.

Melissa's knees went weak. She stayed upright, legs wobbling.

The governor nodded. Elaine turned fast toward her aunt, shock written on her pretty features. Lady Nasibron's gaze swept the aspirants. "Melissa Dorian, are you here?"

Melissa stepped forward. "I am."

By Mother's mercy, I am.

* * *

Lady Nasibron led the five of them through the palace. Elaine followed a short distance behind.

Melissa's stomach still shook and fluttered with a combination of anxiety and relief. The five chosen aspirants met with Governor Lokoth in the palace library several minutes after being announced to the people. Elaine waited outside.

The governor wore a dark-colored formal fencing jacket. She carried no sword but sat, reading, at a desk. Rising when they entered, she smiled. "Lady Nasibron, you've assembled a sturdy group."

Despite liking the man, Melissa would be hard-pressed to describe Hilos as sturdy. She said nothing, grateful for her position and not wanting to risk any of the governor's displeasure.

Lady Nasibron nodded to Lokoth. "Your people are talented, Tandace," said the witch. "I doubt most cities could have produced five candidates who could take a sacra form in mere months. Still, I estimate all five of these have the ability, as do a few others in your new mage unit."

"Impressive work ferreting them all out so fast," said the governor.

"Thank you. I believe you know most of the students already, but I should introduce the others."

"Of course. Go on."

Lady Nasibron motioned to Niu. "This is Niu No Kaewoo, of a Kanori immigrant family. She and her brother both applied, and I think both have the potential to take a sacra form quickly, though Niu should learn faster."

"Excellent," said the governor. "Have you any previous magic experience, Niu?"

Niu flushed, looking at her feet. "No, your serenity."

Governor Lokoth smirked. "All the better."

"Indeed," said Lady Nasibron. "It's better you know nothing, and I have a clean canvas to paint with my knowledge." She nodded, then motioned to the man called Kelt. "I believe you know the other three, but perhaps Kelt of Crayta has escaped your attention. He has been a sailor in the bay for some time, currently a fisherman. While he's not yet a mage, some of his former crew-mates spoke of him as a hero during a past battle with Kanori raiders a few years ago. He can already hear the song of sprites and banes consistently."

Kelt bowed his head. "I am honored to serve, your excellency."

The governor's smirk became a lupine grin. "I'm glad you made it, Kelta of Crayta. I think I recall hearing of a sailor holding the deck of his ship alone in that last battle with Kanor. Was that you, perchance?"

"I know of no other who endured such a situation and lived," Kelt said.

"You have my condolences for your fallen comrades, sailor." Governor Lokoth folded her arms, looking over the five new students. "Each of you is a member of my service now. Suya, Hilos, and Melissa, you already joined yourselves to my government. I take it you will do the same, Kelt of Crayta and Niu No Kaewoo?"

"Just tell me where to swear and what to place my oath upon," said Niu.

Kelt bowed again, gaze on the floor. "Likewise, for me."

Melissa smiled. It was strange, being in a situation where so many were eager to volunteer. She welcomed such strangeness. Her eyes moved to the sword servant, Suya. The woman still carried the governor's long blade in a sheath at her side and a personal sword on the other. When she represented the governor in a duel, she would be allowed to draw the governor's sword in Lokoth's stead.

Many nobility across Tancuon maintained the service of skilled duelists to carry their family weapons. Though Melissa had not seen Suya fight, she doubted the woman would need magic to defeat most human foes. The Vakari warriors, on the other hand, might be a different matter.

"Suya," said the governor. "My sword."

Suya unsheathed the governor's sword, then sank to one knee, presenting the blade to Lokoth, flat across bare palms.

Governor Lokoth took the weapon gently, carefully laying the single-edged weapon upon her arm. "I would have you each swear upon this, the sword given to me by Mother Mercy herself." She wrapped fingers around the hilt and raised the blade slowly over them. "Swear you will serve me loyally under the eyes of Mercy until the day I shall release you of your burden."

"I swear," said Suya, and the others followed her lead. "To serve you loyally, under the eyes of Mercy, until the day you release me of this burden."

Their voices formed a small chorus.

As she spoke the words, Melissa's unsteady stomach stilled. Her mission began this day. Another thought arose unbidden, *today begins a new life.*

She prayed silently as they finished the oath, hoping never to regret her decision in the moment.

Given the governor's generosity, the possibility seemed remote. Given her ambitions, she belonged here. Destiny, wrought of mercy's steel and stone, lingered, almost visible, not far away.

CHAPTER 10

SABEN

Saben Kadias was a man well accustomed to the night. He approached the library in darkness, footfalls soft as cat's paws. His breath, both inhaled and exhaled, sounded no louder than a rustle of leaves in a gentle breeze. He crept around the side of the main entrance and neared the magic wing. Behind him, Jaswei followed in equal quiet. Rond lumbered behind them, surprisingly keeping pace without much additional noise.

The magic wing had no windows, and those on the first level of the main stacks were barred. Saben's inspection on their previous visit made him certain of the security below. However, the second floor was a different story. He braced the sprites in his legs to jump, opening his hands to grab the window-frame once he reached the second level.

Before he could leap, Jaswei held out a hand to stop him. "I'm lighter. Let me."

He frowned, but then nodded. Rond stared at the window. "Don't forget to take what I want."

"That's Jaswei's mission," whispered Saben. "Keep watch."

Rond gave him a shadowy wave of a hand.

"Of course," Saben hissed.

Jaswei leapt to the second floor, her legs boosted by the sprites she'd trained to empower them. Easily grasping the window frame, she drew her bane sword and slashed the lock. Saben caught the outer half of the metal binding before it hit the ground. He stuffed the scrap soundlessly into his pocket while Jaswei pulled the window open and then slipped through it, into the library.

Saben flexed his fingers. He tested the weight of the sword on his back to make sure the weapon was secured in its baldric and wouldn't rattle in motion. Satisfied, he forced his sprites to his legs and leapt. The power coursing through his lower limbs carried him to the window's level. He folded his arms and tucked his head and legs to shrink himself and twisted through the opening. He landed on his feet.

"The way to the magic wing is downstairs," said Jaswei in the ghostly glow of her bane sword.

"Stay ready to fight. The demon guard may still be here."

"Right you are, captain," she said in Najean.

They found their way downstairs in the dark. Saben shrugged off his baldric, set it carefully on the floor, then drew his sword before replacing the baldric on his back. His blade cast glimmers of Jaswei's bane lights on the walls. They prowled through the stacks toward the magic wing, as quietly as they'd moved outside.

Jaswei's gaze followed the flickering light ahead of her. Saben grimaced as he thought of how loud she'd be the next day, one way or the other. She wouldn't be able to keep quiet, scroll or no scroll, after this much silence. Insufferable, but useful, he told himself. He could not have imagined traveling so far across the world without her help.

They reached the door at the far side of the stacks. It wasn't sealed like in daylight. The passage beyond stood open.

"Is that ordinary?" Jaswei asked.

Saben shook his head. "I don't know."

They stared into the gloom beyond the arched doorway. Nothing moved in the magic wing, a place haunted by the secrets of mages and demons. At places likes this, the two orders of life, mortal and immortal, converged. To reach the city above, a human needed one of two things. The first option was to offer utter submission to the rulers of that place. Saben would never give such deference to demons. He grimaced at the thought. The other way to travel to that distant ring was in disguise.

The Tancuonese called their demonic transformations sacra forms. Across the world, the name varied, but the essence and purpose of it were the same. To walk the ring in the sky, to learn the knowledge of demons, and in Saben's case, to find a way to kill such immortal beings.

He gripped the hilt of his sword in both hands. "I'll go first." He stepped forward.

"Then go." Jaswei's voice sounded steady. Still, the sweat shimmering on her forehead and the glimpse of her brittle expression reflected on his sword's polished blade told Saben she was nervous.

He entered the passage with her at his back.

The pair reached the end quickly and quietly. The magic wing's stacks stretched before them. They looked similar to those in the history section behind them, only with racks for scrolls at the end of each shelf. Saben approached the nearest one, reading the label on a metal plaque over the cases, the gold inscribed with flowing Tancuonese script.

He who should read shall learn the ways of the spirit.

"Spells," he murmured as he took in the meaning of the poetry. "They're spells."

"I'll find the one Rond wants," Jaswei said. "You get your sacra form."

"Yes," he said in a low voice. "Take care."

"I always—"

"I know."

She wrinkled her nose at him, then set off through the shadows. As her light diminished, Saben positioned a pair of dark-eater sprites in his eyes. He started to search through the shelves. Perhaps the demon guard was only a myth.

The Tancuonese loved their false securities, from what Saben had seen. Not so different from folk who crafted seals that could command demons with such simplicity, even children could use them.

He gritted his teeth as he remembered his old home. Those seals had not saved them.

At a gap between the central set of shelves, Saben found a stand topped by a scroll case, enclosed in a box of polished glass. His vision sprites allowed him to read the plaque on the side of the box. He read it twice to make sure he understood, first in silence, then in a hushed voice.

"Be wary, magus. Herein lies a scroll of the ascended Azel, scion of Destruction himself."

The word for destruction was written in a stylized fashion, quite different from the rest of the text. The first letter was in high case, and that likely meant it served as a motif name in the local language. Some demons spawned children with mortals or each other, only adding to their numbers and corruption. Destruction himself must refer to an older being than the subject of the scroll. Far more importantly, the motif's name meant this roll of ancient parchment contained a sacra form.

The scroll's place of prominence told Saben that whatever, whomever, the scroll pertained to, it was strong, perhaps strong enough to wage a war in the ring. He'd not expected to recognize the name of the demon he could disguise himself as when he reached this place. Yet, the concept of a son of destruction becoming his to control made Saben's lips curve into a smile.

Jaswei approached him as he examined the glass box, searching for a way to remove it without creating undue sound. She carried a scroll of her own in a case of black wood under one arm.

"This is what Rond wanted," she said.

He grinned, then motioned to the box. "That scroll is what I want."

Jaswei wrinkled her nose. "I can't read the script, but if you say so. Take it, and we'll go."

Saben nodded. He turned from Jaswei, reaching for the box containing the Azel scroll. His fingers brushed the glass, then moved to the side. The box was padlocked. He gripped the metal tightly and tugged, but his strength alone was insufficient to break it. He grunted and stepped back.

Jaswei drew her bane sword in a flicker of light, and the lock broke. Saben caught the broken pieces of metal before they hit the floor, then tucked them into his pocket with the remains of the window's seal. Using both hands, he raised the lid of the box.

He grinned. Light poured across him from behind. Jaswei turned on the spot, bane sword in hand. Saben lifted the scroll and pivoted. The demon guardian of the library stood before them, his pallid greenish skin pulsing with inner illumination.

"Intruders," said the hulking humanoid creature, flexing the fingers of his free hand.

Jaswei shook her head, smiling. "At this time of night? How dare they?"

The demon growled low in his throat.

Saben folded the scroll under his arm. He glared at the demon, then raised his hand, the one bearing the seal of demon control.

The demon laughed before Saben could activate the seal. "Mortal, you know nothing of my kind."

Saben opened his fist. The control seal flared with light. The demon chuckled, shaking his head, then raised a mace with iron rings all along its oblong length. Just like against the demons that destroyed his village, the seal did nothing.

Saben Kadias knew hatred when it grew in his heart. He recognized the fury he felt and saw no reason to dispel it and no way to silence the voices of his slain parents, his missing sister, his lost friends, and his long-destroyed village.

"Jaswei." He grunted, holding the demon scroll out to her.

She took the scroll, then stepped to one side. Saben threw down his baldric, drawing the great sword from it in the same motion. He hurled himself at the demon guardian. His roar of hate-fueled rage echoed through the halls of the library, shaking dust from shelves.

Jaswei leapt backward, landing catlike to weather the force of Saben's battle cry. She averted her eyes as they clashed, the demon blazing bright. Darting to one side, the towering greenish guardian aimed his weapon at Saben's head. He swung his sword overhead as he ducked, cleaving the demon mace in half. His muscles offered protest for only a second as he whirled to cut at the demon's chest. His strike opened a long gash in the greenish flesh. Trickles of pink blood began to well up along the length of the wound.

The demon retaliated with the broken mace, flailing the chain connecting the weapon to his wrist. Saben caught blows on his shoulder and forearm. He staggered under the impact, feeling ruptures inside, that would become bruises, pulsing under his skin. The demon leered at him and brought the broken mace down in another strike.

Saben's blade cut the chain, sending his foe's weapon flying into the stacks of the library with a crash. The throb of internal bleeding ran through Saben's right side. He pressed the attack. As the demon retreated, its meaty fist struck Saben's cheek, driving him off-balance. Despite the blurring and bobbing world he inhabited in the wake of the punch, Saben's sword severed the demon's arm. The creature groaned. He spun to one side, then fell, leaving a pale-red trail.

Jaswei crept to Saben's side. His rage subsided after the battle, though he still seethed with unconcealed, uncontrolled temper. He picked up his baldric, breathing hard, and hung it on his back. Without a word, Saben staggered toward the window where they'd entered. Jaswei caught up with him and offered her shoulder to lean on. He accepted, despite himself. Her firm touch told him she was still on his side.

Good.

They reached the window. He dropped to the ground outside, stiffening his legs with strength sprites to take the landing. The demon's blood dripped from his blade. He cleaned it with a swish of the weapon through the air. Jaswei landed behind him. Rond trundled to meet them.

"No one's watching," he said.

"We should go," said Jaswei.

Saben nodded. The three of them disappeared into the night, carrying the two stolen scrolls. Rond could have his part of the take. The Azel scroll must be powerful, but who could say what Saben needed to take on the demon without a face? The stars overhead reminded him all too clearly of the void of the abomination. That creature had been the target of his first bane roar. The act of crying out had saved his life then, but he doubted it would be enough when next he saw the monster.

The scroll he unfurled when he arrived at the room where he was staying gave him hope. Next door in Jaswei's quarters, everything was silent. Rond was across the hall, probably poring over his prize. Saben Kadias, a man from a village taken by demons, focused on becoming one of them.

The scroll's jagged lettering and bizarre patterns filled his eyes, his mind, and shortly after, his dreams.

CHAPTER 11

MELISSA

Melissa spun the spear and then aimed the weapon's point toward the ground at her feet. She gazed across the small stretch of training yard at Niu. The two of them were among the student-mages training on the palace grounds. Melissa was disappointed by her lack of access to personal training. She'd lacked instruction on magic since she was a young child, and knew she could use the help to catch up with the others.

Yet, Lady Nasibron's insisted on observing all the students at once to gauge their abilities. *Abilities,* Melissa thought, *really what abilities?*

Giles, her brother, had often demonstrated small magical talents when they were young. In the intervening years, Melissa never felt as though she'd been wielding magic until her encounter with the vakari warrior in protecting the governor, and she could hardly recall the sensation from those moments.

Niu advanced toward Melissa, staff in hand, the ends both blunt and reinforced by metal caps. Part of Melissa thought the situation unfair, as she was able to wield the same weapon she'd trained with as a merchant's guard. Niu picked the staff from among the training weapons but looked as though she'd never held one before. They closed the distance and circled each other, testing the range with their long weapons.

Naturally, sprites and banes as Lady Nasibron called them were most able to demonstrate their capabilities when stress drew them out. Melissa recalled such feelings and wasn't pleased with the prospect of facing them again.

She wanted to be a mage as much as she did before. The trials they faced would be difficult for all of them. Despite her fear of demonstrating a lack of magical talent, sparring with a spear didn't stand as stressful for Melissa.

Elaine watched from a distance beside her aunt. She seemed so naive, but also cold and aloof. Melissa disliked the other girl as much as she admired the opportunities Elaine must have benefited from her whole life.

Opportunities like those could have been Melissa's once. The governor favored Melissa with her current prospects, but such blessings were more than the norm. Niu and Melissa exchanged testing strikes.

Even with the spear-point downward, Melissa clearly understood the weight and balance of her weapon better than the other girl. She blocked Niu's blows without much trouble. Niu kept the exercise interesting by changing tact more than once.

At first, she used the ends of the staff interchangeably, mixing up from which direction she would swing. Melissa blocked each strike with alacrity. Niu tried to dart past Melissa and strike straight on with her staff extended in one hand. Melissa ably defended the quivering blow with the spinning shaft of her spear. Niu's extra effort presented little more trouble than her previous flurries of attacks. Melissa tripped Niu with the end of her spear and then pointed the blunt butt of the weapon at her where she lay on her back.

Niu groaned, then shook her head. "You beat me again," she said, "and without magic, too."

Melissa shrugged. "I think I'm missing the point of the training."

Niu frowned. Sweat ran along her brow. "This isn't a real fight. I don't even know what we're supposed to be doing. Does having a winner matter?"

"It matters," Melissa said, "given our positions as favored among the candidates, if we don't demonstrate magical talent, perhaps we'll be demoted."

Niu sat up and shrugged. "I don't like it, but if you think so, that may be true."

"Don't trust me too much," said Melissa with a smile. She withdrew her spear and then offered Niu her hand.

Niu chuckled as she grasped Melissa's hand, then got to her feet. She retrieved the staff from where it lay fallen on the grass. Niu planted one end of the blunt weapon on the grass and faced Melissa. "Honest to Mercy, I did notice something from you."

"Really?" Melissa narrowed her eyes. "What?"

"I think..." said Niu, "...it seemed like you moved faster when I attacked, but also *the song* got louder."

"The song?"

"Melissa, your inner song," said Niu, "It changed like you had a bane song inside."

"I couldn't tell it was different," said Melissa, "what makes you think you didn't imagine it?"

Niu shrugged. "Could have, but I doubt it."

Melissa looked at the spear she held, its sharp end pointed toward the ground. "I don't understand. Shouldn't I hear them too?"

Elaine approached them, clapping her hands together. "I heard some mystic songs in this direction," she said.

"It was Melissa." Niu motioned in her direction.

Elaine turned to Niu. "Thanks, but you made some noise too."

Niu furrowed her brow. "I couldn't hear anything."

"It may be that neither of you is gifted in that way. I had to train for years to hear my inner song."

"Is that so?" Melissa asked.

"It is."

Niu glanced at Melissa. "What were we trying to do?"

"Both you used sprites to enhance your physical abilities," said Elaine. "But, Melissa directed hers with more strength."

"How did I do that?" Melissa asked.

She and Niu both looked curiously at Elaine.

"Questions worth answering." Lady Nasibron approached from out of sight behind Melissa. "I noticed the same among the other three. Promising."

Niu wiped sweat from her brow. "Does that mean? Are we all potential wizards?"

Lady Nasibron nodded. "As possible wielders of sacra forms, you have more possible abilities than you can imagine. Much of the time sprites and banes are trained by your actions. They react to the way you learn."

"All those books," whispered Niu. She shot a glance toward Melissa.

Melissa narrowed her brows. "Could that happen through books?"

Lady Nasibron nodded again. "Likely, it could. If you learn from the written word, you may understand partially the essence of a subject without the material. Without matter, sprites and banes grow as adaptive entities. They adopt qualities from their environment, including the body in which they dwell."

"That explains the advantage Melissa has with her spear," said Niu, "right?"

"That, or you just need to learn to fight." Melissa raised an eyebrow and made a twitch of a smile on her lips.

"Hey!" Niu frowned and Melissa, who smiled, making Niu roll her eyes. "I've only been a library guard for a whole year. Why talk that way?"

"Be calm. This isn't a contest worth having." Lady Nasibron turned to Elaine. "My student, though still in training, is skilled as regards wielding magic independent of physical training."

Elaine flushed slightly. "I understand matching fairly well at present. When a sprite or bane matches the properties of a nonphysical object like an idea or concept from a book it inherits the user's impression of that material as well. That's the basis of spirit-matching."

Melissa smiled. "I read books about tactics and wars from history. I predicted a lot of Niu's moves. You think my sprites helped me fight that way because I read so much?"

Elaine glanced at Lady Nasibron. The elder witch put a hand on her niece's shoulder. "Indeed I do. It's more than possible to improve essences by knowledge without realizing it."

"So, they know what I know better than I do?" Melissa said.

"Yes, on an instinctive level," said Lady Nasibron. "But, they have limitations."

Niu exhaled. "They see what we see and share our experiences. Is all magic just tapping into our past experiences?"

"Half-true." Lady Nasibron folded her arms. "You should not give your instincts too much credence. Sprites and banes are particles you can shape to your will. Instinct only supplies the basics of your abilities. Training along different avenues, not just your inherent traits, is the basis of a mage's craft. Many spells only work because of external sources or other training modifications to your instinctive energies."

Niu pressed a palm to her forehead. "Sounds complicated."

Melissa nodded, energy pulsing with the thoughts racing in her head.

Lady Nasibron's description of sprites and banes excited her. She'd never heard before the nature of the magic's abilities, and limitations explained so deftly. Lady Nasibron was proving herself a good teacher. After the Magister's Guild banned Melissa from study, no teacher in the south would ever train her before.

"Elaine," said Lady Nasibron, "I want you to take these two to the library."

"Me?" Elaine asked.

Lady Nasibron shrugged with a smile. "Student, you are now a senior mage in all ways but for a lack of confidence. Please take these two girls to the library and ask for a selection of mage scrolls. Bring them to the palace. I've heard of an attempted theft at the library over the night, so be sure to take this." Lady Nasibron produced a letter from the governor, the flowering emblem of Lowenrane pressed into the waxen seal.

Elaine took the letter. She nodded to Lady Nasibron. "Follow me." She motioned to Melissa and Niu.

Niu and Melissa followed Elaine from the training yard. They made their way into the city and across the bridges toward the library.

* * *

At the library, behind the front desk, a small librarian waited with an annoyed expression on her weathered face. She glanced toward the inside shelves deeper into the library. A group of soldiers from the city guard were investigating damage to several fallen shelves visible from the doorway at the entrance to one of the other wings. Melissa and Niu approached the desk behind Elaine.

"If you're here for any particular scrolls," said the librarian, "I must ask you to wait until the guards finish investigating."

Elaine said, "Lady Nasibron wishes to see the scrolls of matching if we can."

The librarian hissed a low sound but nodded to Elaine. "Very well." The librarian nodded to Elaine, Niu, and Melissa. "Please follow me."

The three of them followed the librarian around a low barrier and toward guards and the fallen shelves. Blood had dried in places on the floor, looking pale as to be almost gray in the dim light.

Melissa glanced at Elaine. Lady Nasibron's student looked away, aloof as usual. The scene among the shelves was apparently beneath her.

"This way," said the librarian. "You may borrow the scrolls of matching from within. Will that suit you, lady witch?"

"I understand," said Elaine. "That will do."

They picked their way past the guards and retrieved a set of large scrolls the librarian produced from the magic wing's shelves.

* * *

The streets of Soucot were wet with rain when Melissa and the others emerged from the library. She poked her head out from under the eaves by the entrance of the library and held her arm out, feeling for raindrops. Elaine frowned.

Niu glared at the gray sky. "I suppose we'll need to borrow a wagon or a covered cart if we're going to get these scrolls to the palace."

Elaine tapped one toe, folding her arms. "You're right. Can you two find one? I'll stay and guard the scrolls."

"Sure, if you think you need to keep them walking away," said Melissa.

Elaine gave no sign of annoyance but handed Niu a purse of money. "Use this to rent a covered cart."

Melissa and Niu went looking near the library. Melissa glanced over her shoulder as they turned the corner and left the line of sight of the front doors of the library. She glimpsed Elaine leaning to examine the scrolls they'd collected.

Niu and Melissa passed through rainy streets. They found what they were looking for a few blocks from the library. A cart rental stand with the sign out front in Kanori and Tancuonese told them the price was just a few silvers. They approached the dealer and rented the cart with no trouble.

On the way to rejoin Elaine, they came to a side street with a barricade blocking the intersection. People milled around the three large wagons, lined end to end, asking each other who had blocked the street. In the overcast gloom of low hanging clouds, Melissa glanced over the barrier, squinting to see better. Nothing but shadows presented themselves.

"We should go a different way." Niu turned and then pushed their small handcart forward. Raindrops pattered off the covering over her head. Water splashed in places, but the cart's basket remained dry. The two of them proceeded to the street outside the library. A pair of wagons turned sideways in the road blocked that way as well. People pressed against them, looking around for places to find a way through. The other pedestrians looked as confused as Melissa felt.

We just came through here.

Niu pointed through the intensifying rain. "That's a Magister's Guild emblem!"

Melissa frowned. "You certain?"

"Yes!" said Niu. "It's obvious. The trident and the scroll."

The symbol on the supports of the wagon covering was indeed a trident crossing a scroll. It hung on a rope, gold-filigreed metal strapped to the side of the wagon's covering. Melissa approached the symbol and reached for it.

A voice spoke from within the wagon. "Don't touch that."

Melissa paced back a step. "What's going on here?"

"We in the Magister's Guild," said the voice within the wagon, "have our own goals to meet, Melissa Dorian."

Melissa and Niu exchanged glances. Niu grimaced with a nervous twitch in one eye. The two of them retreated from the wagons, then turned to each other.

"They're blocking the road," Niu said. "They must be serious."

Melissa nodded. "They might be after Elaine, as well."

"They should know better than to go after a noble," said Niu.

"Maybe they don't," said Melissa.

"Or maybe they know a way to get away with it." Niu scowled.

The wagons remained before them, impassable. *Is that why they blocked the side street? Is this all a plot to separate us from Elaine and those scrolls?*

"We need to get through there," Melissa said.

"Right," said Niu. "But how?"

"Any way we can move them?"

"Not that I can see." Niu scowled.

Melissa craned her neck. "Can we go over them?"

"We just started training magic," said Niu. "I don't see a way through, especially not with a hand cart."

Melissa frowned. Thoughts of her past magic experience coursed through her head. Neither of them could fly like Deckard Hadrian.

Niu bit her lip. "We need to get past them as soon as possible, right?"

"I'd say so," said Melissa.

"In that case, we could climb."

Melissa shook her head. "They'll be ready for that. And never mind the hand cart."

Niu sighed. "Then, how?"

Melissa rubbed her chin. "Give me a moment to think."

CHAPTER 12

SABEN

Across the street the wagons stood, blocking everyone's path. Saben had observed the library for a night and a day after thieving from the place. He tried to ensure nothing remained behind to jeopardize the identity of his group. They'd decided he should watch alone, at least on the side of the street. On the other side of the library, Jaswei and Rond would be scouting together.

He paused as he spotted two women moving away from the wagons in the middle-of-the-road, pushing a hand cart in the light rain. They appeared agitated and talked to each other with quiet intensity.

Saben approached the pair, wanting to ask what was going on but uncertain if his Tancuonese was up to a conversation with such harried people. Either way, he risked being caught if he shared too much, but he needed information.

They looked toward him as he approached. Saben was a large man, but his usual quiet kept him from being as noticed as Jaswei. He wasn't easily set on edge, but thieving from the library of Soucot had left him in a nervous place. *We ought to leave Soucot soon.*

The taller woman, more Tancuonese in appearance, wore her curly black hair long. Drifting strands at her back emphasized her slender build.

She looked in his direction and frowned, though her eyes remained distant, intent on something in her mind's eye.

The other woman, shorter and curvier and at least partially Kanori in descent, noticed Saben at once. "Hey, what do you want?"

"I want to know what's going on."

"We aren't certain, ourselves," said the curly-haired woman in the language of Tancuon.

The part-Kanori woman shook her head. "The Magister's Guild blocked the street."

"The guild? said Saben, "why?"

The taller woman started to speak but hesitated. Her friend glanced at her, then turned Saben. "We don't know beyond a doubt, but we think they could be after us."

"Why you?" Saben asked. *And a curse on you're appearances for drawing me into a situation I should have avoided.*

"We're members of the governor's new mage guard," said the curly-haired woman. That phrase drew a glance from her friend.

The half-Kanori woman said. "Melissa, are you sure we should tell him?"

"He's not with the guild. Besides, everyone in Soucot will know us soon."

"I'm new to the city," said Saben. "I don't know much but I dislike anyone who restricts magic."

Melissa nodded."For now, don't worry about that. We need to get past those wagons."

Saben folded his arms. "There could be a way around."

Melissa glanced at her friend. "What do you say, Niu? Do we have time to circle around?"

Niu shrugged. "We can't just enter in here."

Saben gazed at the wagons. He took in their heavy bulk, their weighted axles, and their covered beds. Wagons such as these did not usually come so far into the center of a city of Soucot's size. They wouldn't all be here by accident, which all-but-confirmed the pair's suspicions.

Saben turned to Melissa. "I think we'd be better off going through them, even if we cause a scene."

Melissa raised an eyebrow. "We?"

Saben folded his arms and let his voice rumble. "I'm willing to help for a coin or two. I'm new in the city and low on funds."

"So you said." Melissa's eye narrowed and she glanced at Niu.

Niu smiled. "I think we can trust him. And he's got a big sword."

"All right." Her gaze flicked toward his face. "Where exactly do you hail from?"

"I come from a place far to the northeast," said Saben, "I haven't been there in many years." He remembered his village with its burning buildings, ruined gardens, and the complete destruction of all tranquility. "My people aren't there anymore."

Melissa narrowed her eyes. "If I trust you and betray us, I'll make you sorry."

"I'm not some Magister's Guild agent," said Saben, "I've no reason to turn against you."

"Pay me and I won't betray you."

"We'll see that you get paid," said Niu. "We don't have the money here, though. Is that all right?"

Saben unfolded his arms. "If the governor is as good with her gold as you are with your words, there should be no problem."

Melissa turned and glared at the wagons. "The governor may not mind if we tangle with the guild in her service. It's half of our purpose."

Niu nodded.

Saben drew his sword, dropping the sling on the rainy street. He picked up the baldric and replaced it on his back.

"No killing," said Melissa, "all right?"

"No killing," he repeated.

"This is a magic dispute," said Niu, "one between the guild and the governor. We shouldn't bloody our hands over it."

Saben scowled. "But we must defend ourselves."

Melissa hefted the spear-sling at her side. "The best way to do that sometimes is to not escalate. I've been a caravan guard for long enough to know that if someone pulls a knife and the other draws a bow, they're going to continue escalating until one of them runs out of options."

"Magic is on the table then?" Saben asked.

Melissa glanced at him, eyebrows raised. "You're a mage?"

"I have a little talent," said Saben.

Niu's eyes widened. "Then maybe you should lead."

Saben shrugged. "I'm not a wizard, only have the barely a mage in my homeland." *They needn't know about my voice,* he thought.

Melissa, Niu, and Saben approached the wagons. A voice from one of the covered bed called to them. "Go back, we can't let you pass."

Saben raised his sword. "Sounds like a problem for you."

He hefted his sword in both hands and marched straight toward the wagon closer to the library's side of the road. He swung the weapon over his head and brought it down on the axle of the carriage, reinforcing the strength of the weapon with as much power from his sprites as he dared reveal. He cleaved the wheel from the shaft that supported it.

The wagon tilted to one side and spilled its passengers onto the rainy pavement. The stones, slick with water from the increasing downpour, greeted a pile of young guild mages, most of them wearing thin cloaks over their novice uniforms. They hit with groans and cries of pain.

Saben stepped backward, and then paced past them, shoving the side of the wagon. He pushed. Hard. Then he pushed again. The wagon swung to one side, allowing Niu and Melissa to hurry by with their covered handcart. Saben backed after them. As he emerged in the gap onto this street of the library, he turned to follow the women and found himself face-to-face with one of the youths who jumped down from the driving board.

The boy stared at him, eyes fierce. "What are you doing, foreigner?"

Saben slipped the sword back into the baldric, cold, and calm. He reattached the sling to his back and faced the boy with hands folded together, without a word.

The young mage gritted his teeth. "I won't let you pass."

Saben cracked his knuckles and the boy's stare faltered, his eyes turning watery. The student magister backed away a pace, then turned and fled toward the wagons and his fallen friends. Saben marched after Melissa and Niu toward the library, hoping his actions would not draw undue attention to him and his team. Jaswei was usually the one who went out of order and acted as he'd just done. Saben hated his helpful side.

He had a mission, and he needed to continue on that path.

ELAINE

Elaine spotted Melissa and Niu approaching with the handcart. A big man followed them at a short distance. The man caught her eye as one of the novices from the Magister's Guild turned and fled back to their barricading wagons. The giant man with the great sword let the boy go without a word. Elaine waved to them from the doorway of the library. Melissa and Niu brought the handcart to her.

The big man followed them at a slower pace, taking up more room than normally necessary, he blocked the path of any other novice magisters from attempting to go after Niu and Melissa. Elaine met them near the doors. The three of them started to load scrolls onto the handcart.

"Who is he?" Elaine asked.

Melissa shrugged. "A helpful someone," she said, "foreign."

Niu glanced at the man. "I didn't get your name."

"I'm Saben." His voice emerged like a slap of waves on a rocky Charinien shoreline.

Elaine said, "if you helped them, then I owe you one."

"In that case," said Saben, "I suppose you're not the only one who owes me." His voice stayed soft, quieter than she expected from such a large frame.

Elaine folded her arms as they finished loading scrolls into the handcart. She glanced toward the street and the wagons.

"The magister's guild blocked our away back," said Melissa, "It might be difficult to get back to the palace."

Saben glanced at the rooftops, through the falling rain to a woman across the street. She was watching them. "I can help you get back for a small price."

"You're a mercenary?" Elaine frowned at Saben.

He bowed his head. "Fresh from Naje."

"From Naje?" Elaine said, "You've come a long way."

"You could say that." The sound of raindrops almost rendered his words inaudible, despite their wicked growl.

Elaine and the others started into the street, keeping the cover of the handcart pulled low to protect the scrolls. The four of them could get soaked, but the rain must not destroy the ancient scrolls beneath the covering. None of these rolls of parchment belonged to sacra scrolls that wizards used to claim their title. These scrolls contained information that was safer and altogether less esoteric, but also less durable.

The group made it six blocks before the novice magisters got the nerve to follow them. A group of swift-running magister students pursued from behind, while more circled ahead at an even faster clip, accelerated by their resonant essences. The student magisters blocked the road ahead of Elaine and the others from passage.

Saben glanced at Elaine. "You're the leader?"

"I guess so." Elaine's voice sounded high-pitched and brittle in her ears.

"If you let me, I could scatter them all like sheep."

"Do you know much about sheep?" asked Melissa, "because I don't."

"I know sheep," he said softly. "I grew up around them."

"Give it a shot," Niu slowed her pace as another man joined the students in front of them.

"Well, well, well," said the newcomer, who Elaine did not recognize. He wore a mantle that looked too heavy for the summer and stood about seven hands tall. *He's a giant,* Elaine thought, before noticing the mantle flowed longer than his legs. His movement made no sound as he floated above the ground. He positioned himself between the novices ahead of them and Elaine's group.

"I am an elder magister of the guild. It is offensive to me that the governor has chosen to abandon our contract as the keepers of magic in the city. I'll punish those who would defy our order."

Melissa snorted. "What happens if we don't simply roll over for you?"

"We will punish you all the more." The magister's lip curled. The novices behind him exchanged glances and laughter as they advanced to join their master.

Melissa and the others joined Elaine at the front of the handcart. Saben unsheathed his greatsword. He set the baldric on top of the cart, allowing its weight to hold the cover in place. Saben whispered to Elaine, "we should smash through them,"

"How fast can you run?" asked Melissa.

"Fast," said Saben, "Using magic."

"I'm quick too," said Niu, "but I'm not as fast as Melissa."

Elaine stared at the line advancing on them. "You three keep them away from me. I'll get the cart through."

Melissa grunted. "I'm not surrendering, either way."

"Me neither," said Niu.

Saben chuckled, simple and resonant. Elaine glanced at him, but he didn't seem to notice. Instead, he kept his sword in both hands, falling quiet as he advanced toward the novices and the elder mage.

Elaine pushed the cart from behind while Melissa and Niu took opposite sides, preparing their weapons to defend in case of any trouble. Melissa carried her spear and Niu held her staff with both hands. Novices blocked alleyways and closed in from all sides.

Saben broke into a run. Elaine shoved the cart forward as fast as she could go. The four of them raced toward the line of students. Melissa and Niu started lashing out with the blunt ends of their weapons, tripping and battering the young novices over one after another.

They might be mages, but they weren't fully trained yet. Saben carved his path through the center without having to swing his sword. The student magister's parted before him out of fear. Elaine followed him, and the four made their way toward the governor's palace, though it still seemed miles away.

It might only be a few hundred yards to the citadel. Despite Saben's presence, the novices proved bolder and bolder. They darted in closer and hesitated longer before fleeing his reach. She didn't want to see him swing that sword.

The wind shifted, hurling the falling rain sideways. A shadowy shape touched the stones of the street ahead of Elaine.

Melissa shouted, "Deckard, Hadrian!."

The immortal demon hunter stared at the guild mages, sweeping his gaze to encompass all of those present. "Anyone who dares broach the subject of surrendering these scrolls shall answer to me."

Elaine flushed. He's here to help us. Melissa grabbed the corner of the cart to move Elaine faster. They all ran for the palace.

CHAPTER 13

DECKARD

Deckard Hadrian led the way into the vaulted room near the center of the palace. The feast hall adjacent to the throne room offered festivities in honor of different members of society. Today, city guards and sailors thronged the long tables celebrating Kanor's failures to reach Tancuonese shores in their raid since the last war.

Four decades ago, the room would have been used to stockpile resources for a siege. The governor at the time had been devoutly prudent. Tandace Lokoth, unlike her predecessors, was far more ostentatious. Deckard didn't doubt Mother Mercy chose her to succeed the others without reasoning such behavior would be best.

Melissa, Elaine, and the large mercenary called Saben took the lead while Deckard stepped to the side, yet Niu trailed behind, looking at the bright lights, and platters of food on the tables. Hadrian circled back to talk to the former guard, letting Melissa approach the governor by herself. Niu needed to learn to deal with power if she was to survive on her own. Deckard often lacked the time for strays and sad stories. He was, of course, the Lord of Demon Hunters, the Lord of Glass, and many other titles besides, and Mother Mercy's favored tool for scourging rogue demons. Still, he approached Niu.

She wrung her hands together. She was no younger than Melissa but carried with her notably less confidence. Growing up as a girl of foreign descent in the land of mercy could be a cause for caution in many, regardless of their sex. The girl looked up at Deckard's face and he offered her a gentle smile.

"You better hurry, or the governor won't have a chance to thank you for helping bring those scrolls. You don't want to inconvenience anyone, do you?"

She sighed. "The governor doesn't want to talk to me."

"Why do you think that?" asked Deckard. "You're one of her hand now." The Kanori feared reprisal for their people's invasion of this land. However, the people of the land of mercy prized clemency, at least when a foe was defeated. "Be brave as befits a mage."

"She chose me, didn't she," said Niu.

"Yes," Deckard said.

Niu unfolded her hands, with visible effort. She paced past Deckard then glanced over her shoulder at him. "Thank you. I'll do what I can."

She set off to join the others as they approached the governor's place at the party. Tandace Lokoth sat at the head of the longest table, where it stretched into the center of the room. Deckard followed the group toward her. He stayed a short distance away to one side of the feasting hall.

A few warriors and sailors looked in his direction and spoke his name in hushed whispers. He had been a general, commanding troops in the valley to the north, and he'd seen many battles against the Kism and other foes. Deckard saw countless nobles, knights, and commoners lay down their lives for their masters. The war he regretted most was Kanor.

He supposed all who remembered the fighting regretted that last battle in the waters of Charin. The intensity of the conflict had been limited to the sea, but that fact limited nothing. Strife from the conflict resounded for generations. Deckard might be the only man alive in Tancuon to still remember it. Yet, everyone in Lowenrane was still affected, and certainly everyone in Kanor.

Separating them was not enough to keep the rivals from confronting each other again. Deckard thought, *if the and vakari have their way, we'll see more conflict soon.* Whether or not the vakari or the Kanori attacked first, more blood would spill upon the waves.

The governor thanked the three young mages and the newly-arrived mercenary, then told them to take the scrolls to the palace vault. The four left the room, as Deckard approached governor Lokoth. She smiled as he drew near.

"Lord Hadrian." Her eyes glimmered. "I wondered when you'd make your presence felt."

"Your feud with the guild is troublesome," said Deckard.

"You think so?"

"I do." He nodded to the feasting soldiers and sailors. "Do you think they want to go to battle without the help of mages?"

"No one would," said governor Lokoth.

He folded his hands in front of him. "I've met some who disagree."

The governor shrugged. "That's why I'm training my new mage guards and my hand."

"Do you think they will be ready if ships arrive on the horizon from Kanor tomorrow?" asked Deckard.

"My spies suggest Kanor won't threaten us with hostilities for some time, if ever again. You may be paranoid, Deckard Hadrian."

Deckard turned to go, letting the robe move easily around him, it's iron shifted as light as air. He adjusted the metal garment easily, using his magic. His sprites were his most useful as tools in battle, but he used them continuously to hold the robe's weight as well. He stalked toward the doors leading back to the city streets. The governor rose and followed him a few paces.

"Wait, Lord Hadrian," she said, "are you going so soon?"

He shrugged. "I heard at the library, that a particular scroll was stolen."

"What kind of scroll?" asked the governor.

"A demon scroll." Deckard closed his robe around him. "One of the most powerful of its sort, and one I've never faced in battle."

"Many demons are unique," said Lokoth.

Deckard shook his head. "This one is beyond rare."

The governor approached him, where he hesitated beside the table. She asked in a soft voice, "what kind of demon is it?"

He shook his head. "I need to find out more before I can say. It is not the place for mortals to worry about fight a war against the wrath of demons. Especially not this one, if my suspicions hold."

"Are there not mortal hunters," said the governor.

"There are," said Deckard, "but they are not me."

"The same could be said for all mortals, even me. I am not the demon. Nor am I a wizard. I have only a little training."

"You ought to have completed your training as a witch," he said.

Lokoth wrinkled her nose, halfway smiling. "With Lady Nasibron?"

"Perhaps," said Deckard.

Her frown showed the wrinkles on her brow. "There are many things I wish I'd done when I lived in the north. Completing my training with magic is not one of them. I was always better with swords."

"Magic and swords are not always opposed to each other," said Deckard.

"Perhaps, but I'd rather take one over the other. If you understand the meaning."

He nodded at her. "Governor, if it pleases you. I will leave now to continue my investigation."

MELISSA

Melissa turned to the towering foreigner. "What brought you to that street today?"

Saben, if that even was the mercenary's real name, nodded. He took a deep breath. "I didn't know what was going on in sthe library before I got there, but the magister's pissed me off before."

Melissa frowned. "I thought you were new in the city?"

"Judging by your accent. You're not native either," said Saben.

They sat in the palace yard where the other students were practicing, backs to one of the tables. Standing, Melissa stretched her legs. "I was born here. I hadn't been back for some time until now."

Saben said nothing.

Melissa shook her head. "You don't have to talk," she said. "But, given that you helped us, it might be fair to know a little more about you."

Elaine approached them, followed by Lady Nasibron.

"Here they come," said Melissa. "We're in trouble, I guess."

"Why?"

"We're not supposed to skirmish with the Magister's Guild." Melissa wrinkled her nose, annoyed by the governor's order.

Saben scowled without a word. Melissa supposed he really might be resentful toward the Magister's Guild. Even if his grudge against them was a lie, Melissa doubted his motives would interfere with her training. He said nothing.

"Not too talkative now," said Melissa. She waved her hand in the air, motioning toward the witches. "You seem to get along better with Elaine."

Saben remained silent.

Elaine and Lady Nasibron reached them. The elder witch smiled at Saben. "You have been useful today, easterner."

"I suppose so," said Saben.

Lady Nasibron's smiled remained. "What do we owe you?"

Saben shrugged.

"Nothing?" Elaine said.

Saben shrugged again. "I don't know your kinds of money."

Elaine folded her arms and turned to Lady Nasibron.

The older witch said, "we can pay you a few crowns, or a single mercy gold."

Saben closed his eyes. "I'll take the gold."

"Gold it is." Elaine produced a single coin from her purse and handed it to Saben.

He pocketed the heavy yellow disk, then moved to leave. Melissa frowned as Saben turned and walked away.

The mercenary moved her the wrong way, though he'd been useful. Size like his could be valuable in a fight, as long as the man knew how to use it. Still, given his odd mannerisms, she was glad to see him go. Others could accuse Melissa of being quiet, as the other guards sometimes had on the caravan journeys, but she knew her reasons. Women who serve as caravan guards frequently had other problems to attend too far beyond those of the men.

Melissa avoided most of those at the time. In her new life, she'd been asked to form deeper relationships with people. Her service to the governor required more of her than she thought. The position remained a blessing.

Elaine turned to Melissa. "You and Niu did well back there, but you must learn more magic before you cross paths with the Magister's Guild again."

Lady Nasibron nodded. Melissa frowned at Elaine. "I'll try my best, but if I can't avoid them. It will happen again."

"In that case," said Lady Nasibron, "perhaps you should remain in the palace until further notice."

"I'm not going to stay here as a prisoner," said Melissa. "But, I'll try harder to avoid any skirmishes."

Lady Nasibron smiled slightly. "Try as hard as you can."

"And don't go out alone." Elaine crossed her arms. "If the Magister's Guild gets the drop on you, the governor could lose part of her hand."

"I'm part of the governor's hand?" asked Melissa.

"Yes," said the lady witch. "the governor is calling you five training as full wizards her hand."

"Five people for one hand." Melissa smirked. "I suppose that makes each of us a finger?"

"That is the idea," said Lady Nasibron.

"Then what digit does that make you?" said Melissa, glancing at Elaine.

Lady Nasibron scoffed. "Nothing," she said, "she remains my student."

Elaine's face flushed. Some might say her embarrassment was charming. Melissa just felt annoyed.

Despite their training to work together today, her antipathy for Elaine only seemed to grow. Elaine unfolded her arms and turned to walk away. Lady Nasibron shook her head, freezing Elaine in her tracks.

Was there magic between those two just now? Melissa wondered.

Lady Nasibron shook her head again. "Not yet, Elaine."

"What is it?" Elaine asked.

"You have to hear this," said Lady Nasibron. "It concerns every mage in the city."

"Why? Is something wrong?"

"The scroll stolen from the library is most definitely one that we all must approach with concern. I fear its true nature."

Elaine raised an eyebrow. Melissa glanced at the young witch. Elaine usually seemed to exist somewhere between embarrassment and haughtiness, but Melissa sensed for the first time a kind of awe in the young witch. Elaine nodded to Lady Nasibron.

"I will listen," said Elaine. "Thank you."

The elder witch scoffed again. "If one of us should encounter the bearer of that scroll we must do what one can to restrain them. However, our mission is not to deal with the scroll or it's thieves ourselves. We are training for the summer at least, and thus if any of you students should encounter a mage who can wield the power in that scroll, you will be outmatched, as would I."

"Outmatched?" said Elaine. "Even you?"

"Even me," said Lady Nasibron, with a sigh. "I'm an excellent teacher if I must say so myself, but I'm only a middling combat wizard."

Melissa was surprised to hear the old witch make such a statement. Most people, even those who had weaknesses, rarely admitted them. Even students were often trained and kept confident among the Magister's Guild. Melissa recalled as much from the early indoctrination she'd been old enough to attend before being exiled.

"What should we do, my lady?" she asked.

Lady Nasibron snorted. "Do? Run. Run away if you encounter the bearer of that scroll."

Elaine sighed, then turned and walked away. Lady Nasibron didn't stop her this time. She faced Melissa. "Do you understand me, girl?"

"Girl?" Melissa said. "I suppose that describes me, but I'm rarely called so." She smiled.

"Don't get used to it. If you become a wizard, I'll call you by your title instead."

Melissa's smile broadened.

Lady Nasibron motioned Melissa back to training. The elder witch advised the students on how to read the scrolls they'd retrieved, and Melissa worked as hard as any of the others. She went to bed that night tired but satisfied.

CHAPTER 14

DECKARD

Deckard crept between shadows darted under the eaves, before ascending on the wind to glide over the Soucot. He floated silently on the night wind, robe moving as quietly as ever. His dampened essences made certain of that quiet. The robe provided excellent protection in the battle but was also a smooth and supple garment when lightened to the utmost by Deckard's magic.

His vision cut through the darkness and he sensed no unusual songs of sprites or banes beyond those belonging to members of the Magister's Guild, asleep in their homes. A foul smell rose from a building near the docks. Deckard turned in the wind, then glided toward the sea.

He arrived above the docks, casting a shadow beneath the moon as he descended to the street near the largest of the dockyards, an inner harbor near the river's mouth, built for seagoing vessels. Even here, the great ships of the bay rarely touched upon Soucot's docks, of late. Not since the battle with Kanor had foreign trade in the city been prosperous.

The docks of Soucot still thrived for fishermen, who arrived daily to sell their wares for local merchants to take to market. Such food went far cheaper here than in the cities of the north where Deckard traveled more often. The stench his nose caught on the night wind belonged to something far worse than dead fish moldering in an alleyway somewhere. The smell belonged to a demon.

Long ago, Deckard wouldn't trust his nose so much, but after 300 years of hunting demons, he saw the wisdom in following instinct. Sometimes the ears and eyes couldn't provide what he need to track demons walking above the earth. Even powerful demons could suppress their banes songs, and some demons stayed on the surface for years before being hurled down. In distant lands, many demons roamed the surface at will. Deckard was only one man, despite his age and skills.

Hunting demons outside the lands of mercy was far more dangerous than facing them within these borders. Deckard counted his blessings as he landed beside the docks and made his way into an alleyway, following the pungent, telltale, smell of the demon.

He found what he was looking for just a few blocks south of the docks. He made his way to a tangled tenement house, moving soundlessly to reach the second story, and entered the window in the humid night air. Crouching low, he crept through the building, between rooms where some of the city's poorest lay sleeping. He sniffed the air and knew the demon was close at hand. Deckard's nose wrinkled in disgust as he opened the door and found his quarry.

The demon, not much larger than an ordinary dog, looked up at him with the frightened eyes of a lesser hound. Deckard closed the door behind him, and stood before it, blocking the hound demon from bolting as the creature scrambled to stand.

The demon dog was coated in black fur. Bane lights glowed red in streak-patterned running under his fur. Despite his resemblance to an ordinary dog, the demon-possessed long fangs, unlike those of a mortal dog. He licked his chops with a frog-like tongue.

His dark eyes locked on Deckard's face. "Are you a demon hunter?"

"Yes," said Deckard.

The demon huddled, folding his legs, and almost tripped over himself. "Will you throw me down the well?"

The demon's weak, child-like voice suggested Deckard the creature presented no threat. Many demons could be distracting or deceptive, but lesser beings rarely attempted to deceive him. The demon whimpered.

Deckard shrugged. "Stench is not a pit-worthy offense. What brought you to the surface, hound?"

The demon shook like a cold puppy. "I didn't come to the surface willingly."

"You didn't climb up yourself?" Deckard frowned. "Then what are you doing here?"

"I was brought here, but if I tell you who, they would scatter me to the wind."

"They," said Deckard, "that tells me something."

The dog demon whimpered and shuffled, before dropping to the floor and pressing his paws over his eyes.

Deckard sighed. "If it's another rogue demon, I'll take care of them for you. You're doing little harm."

The demon rolled to one side, looking up at Deckard with abject awe. "You would help me?"

"If you help me, then yes."

The dog sniffed the air, and Deckard smiled at him, trying to ease the beast's suspicions. "You aren't you an average hound demon. What are you?"

"I'm unique. My name is Baor. I am not an ambitious demon, just gassy when nervous."

Deckard nodded. "I smelled that. Others probably will, too."

Baor lashed his tail back and forth. "Deckard Hadrian is your name. correct?"

"Yes," said Deckard.

The dog demon whimpered. "Deckard Hadrian, though I can't name the ones that brought me to the surface I can say, they are numerous and powerful." The dog lowered his head and flattened his ears to his skull. "Forgive me. I know little."

"I won't punish you for ignorance. However, you must do something about your smell. I'll be near here for most of the season, at least. I will have another hunter keep an eye on you for now."

Baor bowed his head, bane song weak and soft. Deckard left the tenement and flew into the night.

Deckard approached the palace, wondering about the foreign mercenary called Saben, who had helped the three students escape the magister's ambush earlier in the day. He suspected there was more about the man than he let on. Usually, when someone wouldn't talk, an ulterior motive existed somewhere out of sight. Deckard landed on the balcony outside the governor's chambers.

Governor Lokoth was already asleep, just barely visible through the curtains. Her essences flowed with soft, soothing music. Deckard took to the air once more.

He glided over the palace grounds, searching for someone he could tell of his findings. He put aside any thought of reporting Baor to a mortal demon hunter. Perhaps Lady Nasibron would find someone to keep an eye on the creature. Kellene proved reliable in the past.

He descended, landing outside the witch's study, chambers reserved for visiting wizards of great power. Kellene was a skilled witch and a fine teacher, but as she frequently said to those who she trusted, she lacked some in raw magical power.

Most witches in the Chos Valley, which she usually called home, would embrace her reputation as a teacher. Her name brought wealth and respect to her family, even given her lack of battle experience against the Kism. In the centuries after the conquest of Tancuon, her style of mage became highly valued among the community of mages. Deckard had met countless students of magic over the years, many of whom would have paid dear amounts of coin for a mentor like Kellene Nasibron. Professional tutoring of witchcraft made for a stable existence, far more stable than being a demon hunter, the role Kellene had taken on for some time in her youth.

Deckard tapped on the glass, wondering if she would be up late reading as in past times Deckard met with her. Few others in Soucot stayed up as late. Deckard tapped once, then twice, then three times. On the third tap, the aging witch appeared at the high window in her silken nightgown, face pale in the light from her near-silent illumination sprites. She opened the latch and let him inside, looking more wizened at the late hour, eyelids sagging with fatigue.

Deckard never slept but still understood what it meant to feel exhausted. She could teach him that less all over again, just through her weary eyes.

"Studying?" he asked.

She nodded. "Deckard, what are you doing here?"

He closed the window behind him with a clack of the latch.

"I'm curious, Kellene, as to how you are adjusting, and your students' quality so far."

"Besides the scuffle today?" she said. "I think they're fine. It's only been days since we started recruiting and some have already picked up the basics of matching. A few arrived with some knowledge in addition to their talents. Most don't know what they're doing, or what they must do to learn faster." Kellene frowned. "Is that all you want to ask me in the middle of the night?"

"Almost so," said Deckard. "Just one more thing."

"Go ahead, then." The witch's lip curled, though her eyes remained tired. "Or do I have to drag it out of you?"

"You won't have to drag anything anywhere."

"Good, thing too. As my years grow, I like the idea of hauling your luggage around with me less and less."

Deckard half-laughed, but stifled the sound with his hand, so as not to disturb others sleeping in the palace.

"In that case, I'll be brief. There's a dog demon hiding near the docks. He is harmless, but you may want to keep an eye on him. His name is Baor..."

SABEN

Saben and rejoined the others in the dead of night. They met at the street corner outside their inn, not far from the harbor's innermost docks. Saben had taken the long way to get back, yet Jaswei still waited up for him. She waved in his direction as he approached. They brought their heads close together to talk. Rond keeping a lookout from the shadows nearby.

Jaswei asked, "What happened today?"

Saben grunted. "That's my question, too."

"All right." Rond stopped closer. "But what happened?"

"Why do you care?" asked Saben.

"I'm part of the team," said Rond.

"You're new to use." Jaswei's gaze flicked from Rond to Saben. "Don't get ahead of yourself."

Rond folded his arms. His belly looked even more thick and round in the moonlight. "You don't have any call order me around, girl."

Jaswei turned, one hand on the sheath with no sword held in it. She stared like a blade's point at Rond and he fell silent. "Like a trap and a trick." She smiled at Saben. "What's the news?" she added in Najean.

"The scroll is safe," said Saben. "I think we are too."

"If we stay out of trouble, we'll be fine, but you didn't keep free of attention today."

Saben grimaced. "You're not going to let me forget that, are you?"

"Of course not," said Jaswei.

"Good." Saben bowed his head. "I was foolish."

Rond shook his head, teeth gritted. "You can say that again."

"What made you want to help those women?" Jaswei asked.

Saben shrugged. "I thought I'd get some gold for it."

"What made you think you would get paid at the time?"

"They looked moneyed," said Saben, but he honestly hadn't guessed as much at the time.

"We could use more. Did you get paid?"

"Yes."

"Good," said Rond. "I'm not filled up with coins, you know."

"No one asked for your words," Saben said with a hiss of contempt.

Rond scowled art him through the shadows. "I don't know why I bother."

"You want a part of what we're doing," said Jaswei. "Or you wouldn't."

Rond's hurt and anger deepened the tempestuous lines on his face, but his rage stayed impotent, despite his expression.

Saben shrugged. "You are new to the group, but we'll split the money with you. We'll pay what we owe."

Rond startled, smiled quickly, and then laughed. "Are you trying to buy me out?"

"Buy you out?" Jaswei wrinkled her brow. "What do you mean?"

"You're trying to settle up accounts with me, so you can leave behind, is that it?"

"If you're not fit to work as a mercenary, that would be best." Jaswei glanced at Saben.

Saben shook his head. "I wasn't trying to settle accounts with you. Your Tancuonese is growing quickly, Jaswei."

"I practiced a lot while you were away." She winked at him.

Rond grinned. "Perhaps you owe me for that as well."

"Don't think yourself lucky," said Saben.

The minstrel chuckled. "Fine."

The three entered the inn, walking upstairs to their accommodations.

MELISSA

She woke to the sound of birds fluttering and calling outside her window. Dressed in her training gear, then went to her balcony, which adjoined her room and Hilos' new student quarters. Melissa peered into the daylight. Crows fluttered all over the yard, a flock of countless birds.

She frowned, as she recognized them as more northerly creatures. They shouldn't be so far south. *Something must be amiss.* The flock moved as one, shifting like a living thing. Turning, she glanced across the balcony as Hilos stepped out his door.

"What are they doing?" she asked.

He frowned. "I take it they're messengers."

"Crows?" said Melissa. I'd not known of any crows to fly so far south."

"Those are no ordinary birds."

"Who could send a flock of birds as a messenger?" Melissa asked.

"I think I know," said Hilos. "I'm afraid it is beyond my ability and station to tell."

Melissa frowned. "Your station?"

"I don't know if it's proper to tell you where these birds came from."

"You are still a gentle servant," said Melissa, "At least, officially."

"I serve the governor." They glanced at each other, and he smiled. "I'll tell you once I'm allowed."

They each went back into their separate rooms. At least, the former knight seemed honest about why he couldn't discuss the birds further.

I'm going to be kept in the dark about most things, being a mere peasant to these people.

Her parents had been merchants, but she wasn't one any longer. She had few mementos of her upbringing, and most of them were painful.

Melissa wandered the palace, as today was the hand's break from training. Though she'd achieved a certain degree of control over her essences, she had not yet found a concept that directed them. Everything she tried only created a mass of pain within her, combined with disappointment at the ineffectual movements of her sprites and banes.

She reached the yard outside and found Niu practicing with her brother.

Niu glanced in her direction. "Melissa," she called. "Want to practice?"

Melissa felt her aching back, still stiff from strikes suffered during earlier sparring. "I'm still hurting from the last three days."

"Oh, I understand," said Niu.

Tal smiled. "If you lack stamina, perhaps you could use more physical training as well as magical practice."

"What did you have in mind?" Melissa snorted.

"Well, you know," Tal said, "running, fighting...something else?"

"I think I've had enough of all that for now."

He flushed and turned to Niu, who shook her head. "Please stop being ridiculous, brother."

Melissa stretched with both hands pressed to her back. "I'd rather rest than train, to be honest."

Niu nodded. "We should take a break as well."

She and Tal joined Melissa as she walked toward the gates of the palace's outer yard. They left the citadel and entered the marketplaces beyond the walls. With the three of them together, the Magister's Guild might seek to bother them. If they encountered hostile magisters, their directive was to flee. Melissa finally understood the challenge of using magic, so she could swallow her pride for the moment.

In the market, they bought food from a few different vendors and ate at one of the small covered stands by a well that served the passersby clean, fruit-infused water. Except for the taste of apples in the water, the market proved almost like any other in Tancuon, even ones far to the north. Soucot reminded Melissa more of her childhood even as the taste of infused water pleased her tongue. People in the north milled around less, but here everyone relaxed more in their pace.

Melissa and the others finished their food, then made their way back toward the palace along a road leading past a divinity college dedicated to the clergy of Mother Mercy. The school's gray, imposing, stone walls cast a long shadow.

A College of Mercy made an imposing centerpiece for many northern towns, but in the south, it looked even starker. The churchgoers and students made their way in and out as the three of them passed. The college appeared to be thriving, which could be because of the governor's presence in the city. Governors were picked by Mother Mercy, so it was said, one by one, hand by hand.

Hand, Melissa thought, *now I'm part of the governor's hand. In a way, I have been blessed by Mother Mercy directly.*

At the palace, they found the flock of crows still circling low over the yard. Lady Nasibron walked beneath the birds, calling to them in a loud voice, speaking a language Melissa did not understand. The birds descended in wide circles, landing upon trees around the edge of the yard. Lady Nasibron approached a cluster of them, black gown billowing around her.

Melissa glanced at Niu. "Want to find out what they're doing?"

Niu's brows bent and she tapped her lip with her finger.

Tal frowned. "Those birds move as if they're one creature."

"I suspect they may be," said Melissa.

"How?" asked Niu.

Melissa nodded. "I remember reading a book once, about a place far away, where demons could take the forms of animals."

"Demons can take the shape of animals?" Tal froze in his step, gazing at the trees dark with crows.

"It could possible. I mean, wizards take on demon's forms," Melissa said. "In the book, they could split into more than one animal at a time, too."

"I'd like to know how many animals make one demon," said Tal.

Niu rolled her eyes. "Brother, you'd question the destroyer himself if you met the beast."

Melissa laughed. "In the book, there were pictures like this, where a group of demon-animals and a single person could keep a conference together, though the pictures in the book showed wolves."

"That sounds an interesting book," said Niu. "But I've never heard of anything like that."

Melissa shrugged. "You're seeing it now."

"What language is she speaking?" asked Tal.

Niu shrugged. "None that I know."

Melissa shook her head. "Same for me."

Tal frowned and then started walking toward the flock of birds and Lady Nasibron

"Don't get too close," Niu said.

"It'll be fine," said Tal.

Melissa followed Tal toward the birds and the witch and found his guess incorrect.

Lady Nasibron turned and glared at them. "Stand back, students."

"I'm part of the hand of Lowenrane's serene governor," said Melissa.

"And you're my student, sadly," said Lady Nasibron. "Now, go back."

Melissa continued forward. "I'm not your student by choice. I'd take any teacher."

"I'm the one you have," said the old witch. "Don't fight me, please."

"Please?" said Melissa, "we just want to know what that thing is doing here?"

"That thing," said the voice of countless birds squawking from the flock, "is a demon."

"A demon," said Melissa, "I was right!"

"You were correct. So go back, before I lose my patience."

The bird demon spoke as a multitude of voices. Melissa and Tal listened to the words this time, retreating at once.

CHAPTER 15

SABEN

Saben, Jaswei, and Rond crept through the alleyway, three days after stealing the scroll. The daylight already waning, they made crept through the alleyway to a door on one side. The wooden structure of the building rattled when Saben knocked.

A slat opened in the doorway. A pair of eyes peered out at them. "Who goes there?"

"My name is Saben Kadias." He motioned to Jaswei and Rond. "We are foreigners."

"What do you want with us then, foreigners?"

Saben grimaced. "We're also mercenaries."

Jaswei grinned at the eyes regarding them from behind the door.

"Are you looking for work?" asked the voice.

Saben glowered through the slat. "Yeah."

The door creaked open. The man behind it stood little taller than a dwarf and wore a shaggy red beard. He motioned them inside, rubbing his bald pate with his hand. The moment all of them were inside, the short man coughed into a handkerchief. Saben tried to ignore the traces of dark fluid on the cloth as he and the others walked past the door guard, into the small room. He stooped to fit under the low ceiling.

Saben and Jaswei took seats on the far side of the room near another door that led into what must be the center of the building. Rond paced back and forth despite the presence of a third chair. The red-haired man walked between Jaswei and Saben and knocked on the inner door, which immediately swung open. He motioned for Jaswei and Saben to rise, then led them inside. What remained of his red hair, bounced in tufts on his head as he walked.

The tavern room had a higher ceiling and was arranged specifically as a dive for recruiting mercenary muscle. The tables were all small and private. Boards with papers scrawled with Tancuonese and Kanori writing lined the walls and support pillars throughout the room. Whoever ran this place must understand the danger of operating in the land of mercy without a holy dictate. The four of them reached the bar.

A man even taller and thicker than Saben, with a brutally blunt nose turned and glared at them over a mug of ale. "You brought us new recruits," the giant said to the little man.

"The big guy looked like he could be useful," said the door guard.

The big man set his mug on the bar. "These others aren't as promising."

Jaswei snorted. Rond folded his arms. Saben rolled his eyes, holding back a curse at the bar man's ignorance.

"What kind of work are you looking for?" asked the barkeep.

Jaswei stepped forward. "We specialize in thievery and violence."

"Violence?" The big man barked a laugh. "You serious?"

"Quite." Jaswei grinned.

Rond huffed but said nothing.

Saben nodded. "They don't look the part, but she speaks the truth."

"That one's a minstrel," said the dwarf, point at Rond.

The towering barman nodded. "I've heard him play once. Sounded pretty good. Why go to the blade?"

Rond blew air out his nose in a derisive copy of Jaswei's earlier snort. The exaggerated breath whistled through the room. Bleary eyes turned from their tables and looked at them. Rond folded his arms and glared at the man behind the bar. "I prefer to cross my opponents."

"Your opponents?" The big man shook his head. "You three are all interesting, but you big man, you look strong. Fat man does not."

"I'm plenty strong," said Rond. "Ask anyone."

The big man rolled his eyes. Saben couldn't help but silently agree with him. He hadn't seen Rond do much beyond talk, though words could be useful in their own way. Of course, Jaswei liked to talk even more, and she was picking up Tancuonese fast.

Jaswei glanced at the little man with the red hair. "You got us in the door. Thanks."

The little man laughed. "It's my job."

Jaswei shrugged. "You did it well."

"What's that supposed to mean?"

Jaswei shrugged. "It may not mean anything."

The little man shook his head. "Be that way, then."

Saben turned to the little man. "What she means to say is she's still new at speaking your language."

The little man's eyes narrowed for a moment before comprehension's dawn broke on his face. Saben and the others turned back to the big bartender. The door guard scurried back to the anteroom. Around them, other mercenaries turned their attention back to their drinks and talk. The low hum of conversation returned from the shadowy corners.

The man behind the bar nodded. "My name is Eric," he said. "I'm the broker here."

"So you broke things?" said Jaswei.

"I don't break anything."

Saben motioned to the mug on the bar. "Especially not the glasses."

"I'm a careful dealer. Too valuable to go breaking cups. Everything here is precious, except life."

"Is that some kind of motto?" asked Rond.

"It is what it is," said the barkeep. "Do you three want a job, or what?"

"If one suits us," Saben said.

Eric motioned to a board of tattered papers on one wall with a massive hand. "Those are the old jobs, still unfinished." Then he waved to a board on the other side of the room, one with fewer papers on it, each held in place by a gleaming metal nail protruding from the wall rather than pounded into it. "That wall is for magic work."

Saben glanced at Jaswei.

She smirked. "Magic work suits u."

Saben bowed his head to her. He wanted the opportunity to try out the power of his new demon scroll. If he didn't get that chance from work as a mercenary, he would, with luck, gain enough coin to secure a place for practice.

"Now, don't get too hasty. There's a lot of work out there for those law-abiders who want to capture people doing unsanctioned magic right now. Some damn scroll got stolen from the city library."

"I heard about that," Rond said.

Eric laughed. "Who hasn't?"

Jaswei and Rond both glanced at Saben. He folded his arms. "We want a magic job as soon as possible. I have to know what the land is like here."

"You're a bold one, foreigner." Eric paced to the end of the bar, motioning them onward to the wall of magical writs. The papers were not themselves magical, but the nails most definitely contained bound essences, from which issued soft songs. Binding sprites kept the writing from being read at a distance.

Saben had seen many tricks like theses in the land of the northeast, but in those days his sense for essence songs had been less keen. Secrecy ranked among the most practical tools of mercenary work. He and Jaswei chose a writ from the wall and returned to a table where Rond read the script for them. Jaswei illuminated the table with a single sprite's glow. Rond dug into the writ, examining every detail, then translated the job to them.

The local proves himself useful, Saben admitted without a word. Not reading Tancuonese would become a significant drawback without the minstrel.

"The job is to retrieve a bell invested with magic, I guess. But it looks like everyone who has attempted it before has been seriously hurt or killed." Rond looked up at Saben and Jaswei. "Does that sound good to you?"

* * *

The three of them used the last of their gold to buy a wagon and took it along the northern branch of the road leading away from Soucot. Among the orchards, lay a single tomb, one belonging to a fallen hero. Saben didn't know the name of the hero but had learned at the bar he was some knight from ages past. *Some heroes apparently can be forgotten.*

They arrived at the gates of the walled mausoleum standing above ground and the wagon ground to a halt.

Saben and Jaswei made their way inside, leaving Rond with the wagon and the mules pulling it. The two of them would be enough to clear any dangerous magic in the area, and Rond would be a liability in a fight with a supernatural creature. *A demon,* Saben thought, *would be the perfect test of my powers.*

He and Jaswei reached the mausoleum beyond the gateway. The doors stood open behind them, moving gently in the wind. Iron bars creaked.

Jaswei looked at the doors of the tomb itself, but it was sealed and locked. "WE may have to break the archway if we want to clear the curse."

"Maybe not," said Saben.

She arched an eyebrow.

He met her gaze. "It looks as though this place may not house the relic, though it could be nearby."

"Why do you say that?" asked Jaswei.

"You can hear them," said Saben, "the sprites?"

She inclined her head and listened for a moment. Saben focused on his hearing as well.

Sprites seemed loud to him when humans weren't talking. A tremulous song issued from behind the mausoleum, from a walled garden in the area beyond the gates. He turned Jaswei.

She frowned at him. "I don't hear anything."

"I must've sharpened my ears recently," said Saben. "Typically, things go the opposite way. We should examine the garden out back before we go inside."

"A good plan," said Jaswei.

They circled the mausoleum to reach the garden. Roses and thistles clumped together all-around a small pond, contained like a reflecting pool within a ring of stones. Plants along the edge of the water had overgrown their places and the stalks of flowers broke through the bottom of the gate before them. Fragmented sprites and banes floated among the flowers, but no song came from these ruins of magical essence.

Saben approached the water, crunching his shoes through the flower bed. That soft essence song he'd heard by the tomb emanated from the pool. Thorns pricked at his heavy gloves but didn't pierce them. Jaswei hung back a short distance. The two of them peered into the water. The pool glittered silver at the bottom, and the sprite song resonated on the rippling surface.

Saben glanced at Jaswei. "The song is coming from in there."

Jaswei frowned. "I can hear it a little." She joined him at the water's edge. "It's in there."

He nodded. "It doesn't look deep."

"Perhaps one of us should tell Rond," said Jaswei.

"Not yet. We must keep alert—"

"And test the essences here, yeah." Jaswei pulled her weapon sprites and banes from the empty sheathe into the air, shaping them to form a small net. Once she completed her snare, she cast the essences into the water. The net sank, gently covering every span of the tiled pool to search out signs of traps and poisons.

The essences raced back to Jaswei, leaving no trace of any disruption in the pool. She shook her head. "Nothing there."

Saben folded his arms and peered into the water. "There has to be something."

Jaswei gazed at the water. "Perhaps touching the surface physically could trigger something?"

Saben nodded. "Perhaps."

Jaswei backed away from the water's edge. She glanced at the mausoleum. "Could the building be just a distraction?"

"Possibly," said Saben.

Jaswei frowned. "If that's the case, then perhaps people would have tried to open it before?"

Saben's brows kit together. "You mean? They were misled?"

"And we were as well, yeah."

If they were misled to come to this pool, perhaps the water itself was the trap. He turned from the paved pond and found Jaswei already a step ahead of him, facing a shade, a figure materialized of pure banes from fragments remaining around the pool. Behind them came a hiss of steam. He glanced over his shoulder and found another spirit composed only of sprites singing loud, terrible notes.

"These two guard the place, is that it?" he muttered.

"By killing intruders." Jaswei reached for her scabbard and drew her sword banes from it.

Saben glared at the bane construct before him. The specter's silvery hands clasped together, then spread, turning into wicked daggers before his eyes. Fingertips long as Najean roofing-nails.

Jaswei charged at the bane specter, her sword of singing essence flying before her. Saben lacked the room to swing his heavy sword, so he cast about to mutter a curse. As the sprite construct closed with him, he released a bellow that repelled the attacker violently. The explosive sound, focused from his voice, smashed the specter to piece. Saben turned as Jaswei finished the bane construct with a swipe of her sword. Her blade cut easily through it, spreading its internal particles like butter.

"That was easy," said Jaswei.

"Don't speak so fast." Saben turned as the sprite construct he'd blown apart reformed, pulling pieces together again.

The bane specter shuffled its body back into one piece, drifting toward Jaswei. Saben and Jaswei fought back to back, defending themselves with the striking essences of Jaswei's blade and echoing shouts from Saben creating a din of combat.

The two constructs remained equally undeterred by both methods of battle. They attacked with surprising vigor, despite being ghostly wraiths.

They're like the creatures from the other side of the bay, the hauntings.

He wished his shout was as effective against these as it was against the water haunts. He scattered the sprite specter with a swing of his arm, but the ghostly claws latched on. The nails of blood-drinking talons pierced his flesh.

He shouted straight into the creature's face, blasting the construct into pieces once more. His arm bled heavily. Jaswei whirled, having sliced through the bane specter once more. Sweat began to bead on her brow. She would tire, as would Saben, before long. Him, especially, now that'd he'd been wounded.

The ghosts lacked such a weakness.

"What we do?" asked Jaswei.

"Perhaps we retreat," said Saben.

"Good idea. We need a plan."

They raced from the pond, toward the enclosure's gates. Both constructs gave chase. Moving with astonishing speed, the two specters cut off the path of escape. Jaswei and Saben face them side by side, rather than back to back.

"We can't seem to hurt them," said Jaswei.

"Agreed," said Saben, "what would you suggest?"

Jaswei scowled. "We need a way to destroy them for good."

"Any ideas?" asked Saben.

"Just one." Jaswei extended her bare arm to draw in the attack of the bane construct. Claws raced toward her, just as sharp and lethal as those of the sprite construct that had torn gashes in Saben's arm.

She let the talons strike her arm and shoulder. Blood dribbled from the wounds, even as the blades sank in. She did not pull back or cut to the spirit with her blade, but reached out with her other arm and separated banes from one another, along the construct's shoulder. He watched with sickened awe.

Jaswei plucked at the essences, her teeth gritted, until the arm of the bane construct loosened, then fell apart. Saben seized his chance and pulled the separated banes into his blade and then into his body.

He drank the bane construct's power as the ghost howled in pain. Jaswei sank to the red-dabbled grass, blood running from her wounds.

Saben rushed to attack the wounded bane construct. He swung his arm and caught the thing about the neck. He pinched his fingers and dragged banes apart one by one, with intense concentration etched on his mind and heart. The bane spirit disintegrated completely after he took the banes from its head.

The sprite ghost attacked, slicing forward to strike at Jaswei. Blades stabbed into her unwounded arm, drawing more blood from her.

Saben whirled, drawing his sword. He thrust the weapon into the remaining construct before the baldric hit the ground. His sword carved through the ghost like it wasn't there at all. The ordinary steel he focused his essences through allowed him to draw the sprites out of the specter and trap them in the blade. The construct collapsed into nothingness.

He reached Jaswei's side, pulling out the bandages he kept in his baldric. He wrapped them around her arms, but she was already lying on her side, eyes closed, and breathing shallow. She'd been hurt far worse than him by the construct guardians. Once he stopped the bleeding, he lifted her in his arms and carried her toward the wagon.

He stopped before he could leave the gates. The constructs had been fresh, which made him guess if the two of them left this place, the guardians might reform completely. The walls might even bind the specters' sprite and banes to keep them from escaping. Peering at them, he found the walls etched with magical sigils. Those signs and symbols kept essences from harming the stone, trapping the two constructs inside these walls as long as the relic remained.

Mortals could pass, but spirits remained imprisoned with the prize. He set Jaswei's unconscious form on the grass, then approached the mausoleum's inner doors. Jaswei's breathing behind him remained shallow, but he still could hear it, even so far away. Her unusual talents kept her alive for the moment.

Saben took his sword in both hands and smashed the pommel upon the gate's inner lock, shattering it with one blow.

He pushed open the iron doors of the mausoleum. They were corroded with rust and moved slowly, but still allowed him inside. Stodgy air flowed into his nostrils from the darkness within. Bones and skeletal wrappings littered the floor.

A single glowing shape lit the space before him, a glinting silver bell upon a pedestal in the center of the mausoleum. That bell was the relic he and Jaswei had been tasked with recovering. They'd make a pretty penny, as long as they could return it to the city alive. Saben reached for the bell.

CHAPTER 16

ELAINE

Elaine watched the bird demon from her window. The palace was growing tiresome quickly,, but thankfully that demon's presence was not hers to worry about. Lady Nasibron was taking care of it.

No doubt, that was Calferis, the bound demon from her household. That demon had watched over Elaine for her whole life.

The bird demon took deep breaths, issued squawks from many beaks, and then fluttered away, leaving Lady Nasibron standing below. Elaine hoped the message hadn't been a complaint about her. She'd only sent her most recent letter home yesterday.

Lady Nasibron returned to the palace. Elaine watched her enter through the door,s then turned from her window. Elaine wanted so much to do something besides train these recruits. Melissa Dorian disliked her immensely, though Elaine only wanted both of them to get along, so maybe she could have an actual friend in the palace.

Outside in the hallway, the gentle servants were mopping up the floor from some spilled water.

She spotted one of the other members of the governor's hand, the former sailor, Kelt Crayta. He was not holding his oar this time but carried a mop instead. He swung the broom-end in the air, obviously having-borrowed the tool from the gentle servants while they worked.

His rippling shoulders moved with ease, shifting flawlessly to wield the broom upright or down low. He glanced at Elaine as she walked toward him. "See anything interesting?"

Elaine shrugged. "You need more technique," she said. "You clearly already have the muscle."

Kelt smiled. "I think you missed the intent of my question."

"Oh," said Elaine, "you didn't want my criticism? I thought you asked for it."

Kelt sighed. "I was referring to my technique. That's for certain."

Elaine rolled her eyes. "I take your meaning now." She walked past him, ignoring his sputtering reply.

Of all the people she met in the city, the only one who seemed both helpful and reasonable had been that mercenary, Saben. Elaine doubted she'd see the quiet man again. He was likely of some ill-repute, given his lack of presence at the palace among the mages the governor recruited. If he proved more worthy, she might have liked to see him again.

Elaine entered the front hall of the palace and found her aunt standing on the ground floor at the bottom of the three staircases. A slim woman in black approached, alone and confident from the throne room. Lady Nasibron turned and met Governor Lokoth with a bow. Elaine decided she didn't care what they had to say to each other. She didn't intend to listen in on them. This palace belonged to the governor and Elaine stayed with her aunt, only at the honored woman's pleasure.

I must insist on this building not become my prison. Elaine proceeded down the stairs, past the governor, and her aunt, and out into the open air. She spotted Melissa, Niu, and Tal approaching from the citadel gate.

She frowned, not wanting another altercation with Melissa. That woman was too unreasonable to see Elaine only wanted to be friends.

It almost makes sense with her history being so problematic, Elaine thought. Still, it would help to know the specifics of the troubles Melissa had suffered. Living in Soucot obviously did not sit well with either of them.

MELISSA

Melissa spotted Elaine ahead of them as she and Niu approached the gates of the palace. She frowned apprehensively, considering the aloof and haughty Elaine waiting for them. At least they weren't being chased by a crowd of magisters this time.

"Welcome back," said Elaine.

"Thanks," said Niu.

Melissa wrinkled her nose. Tal glanced in her direction before nodding to Elaine. "We were out getting food, my lady."

"Food?" Elaine asked. "Isn't there enough in the palace?"

"It's different in the city."

"I'm surprised you'd want to go into the city," Elaine said, "considering what happened last time we went without a chaperone."

"It was fine. I don't need protection," said Melissa.

Elaine shrugged. "If you say so. Personally, I don't think it a risk worth taking."

Melissa glared at her. "You aren't in charge of any of us. You're a student too!"

Elaine retreated a pace at Melissa's outburst. Her face flushed, and her eyes narrowed. "I didn't intend to enforce anything on you."

Melissa shook her head. "Seems to me that your intentions have very little in common with what you do."

"What is that supposed to mean?" said Elaine, cheeks red. "I know how to control myself."

"Well, if the boot squeaks, it'd be your voice," said Melissa. "I've never met anyone so erratic."

"Erratic? I'm not erratic!" Elaine scowled at Melissa.

"You're erratic. That's settled." Melissa grimaced.

"I'll take that to mean you've grown comfortable enough to criticize a noblewoman."

"So you'll play that card now? I suppose I have. Thanks much."

"Melissa," said Niu, "please, give it a rest."

Melissa glanced at Niu. "Point taken." She turned to Elaine. "Just stop acting like you're in charge. Even though you aren't trying to act like you're in charge."

"What does that truly mean?" asked Elaine.

"I'm sick of having to put up with your innocent act," said Melissa. "You're almost a full witch, so act like one. Scheme if you need to scheme, but don't go around acting like you're just some naïve girl."

Elaine looked at her feet. "Sorry," she said. "I..."

"Okay, so maybe you are just lonely. Maybe that doesn't matter to me." Melissa's heartbeat quickened and she spun on her heel.

Elaine sputtered as Melissa walked past her. Fuming, Melissa climbed the stairs toward her chambers. Her footsteps thumped in the hallways, attracting attention from not only the gentle servants but also the birds on the windowsills. She slammed her door and sat on the bed.

I shouldn't be so angry but she shouldn't have pushed me. I didn't even realize how tense I was before. Melissa put her face in her hands. The door creaked open, and she looked up to see Elaine standing just outside. Melissa's eyes misted with tears.

* * *

Melissa and Elaine sat in silence for some time. While they did, Melissa let a strange sensation of forgiveness and shame wash over her. She had taken her dislike of Elaine too far. Now, she owed the noblewoman an apology.

An apology? Melissa shook her head at the thought. She had nothing to offer to apologize to someone who already had everything she could want.

Elaine sat in the chair, the same one Deckard had occupied when Melissa first awakened in the palace. "Elaine," she said, "I'm sorry."

"I see what you meant, though. I have been condescending to you."

"No," said Melissa, "I overreacted."

"I don't know what I did to make you upset," said Elaine. "I only hope you don't feel that way again."

Melissa gritted her teeth. As if Elaine being better and more gracious on top of everything helped. She worked to straighten her expression, easing her jaw. "I'm sorry. I shouldn't have yelled and insulted you."

Elaine smiled. "Well, it's over now. I can help you train. If you want."

Melissa frowned, thoughtful. "I can't always command my essences. They always overreact, a little like me."

Elaine covered her mouth with her hand. "I can help you with that," she said. "I had trouble with my sprites at the start as well."

"You had trouble matching?"

"Yes," said Elaine. "I'm far from a swift learner when it comes to magic."

"I learn most things quickly," said Melissa, "Everything but magic."

Elaine smoothed her skirt. "Think nothing of our exchange earlier."

Melissa finally smiled. "All right, so what should we do?"

Elaine stretched with one arm and shrugged. "Well, we can't go outside for the moment. I think Calferis is still out there."

"Calferis?"

"The bird demon," said Elaine. "I'm sure you saw him."

"That flock of crows?" said Melissa.

"Blackbirds," said Elaine. "Not any particular kind. He has been in service to the Tanlos family for a long time."

Melissa arched an eyebrow. "A demon serves your family?"

"Yes," said Elaine, "the whole flock is one being. Calferis serves for my father, as he was bound to his family generations ago. He's never liked me, though."

"Serving the same family for generations? I could see that getting old."

Elaine rolled her eyes. "My father treats him well, but mortals can't handle his kind."

"Right," said Melissa. "I can't imagine having an immortal follow me around."

"Or anyone, really?" said Elaine.

Melissa turned to look out the window and over the balcony. What Elaine said made sense, but Melissa didn't like facing the knowledge she had been driving people away from her for a long time.

"Let's talk about magic," Melissa said, "shall we?"

Elaine got out of Melissa's borrowed chair. She walked to the foot of the bed. Turning to Melissa, Elaine folded her hands. "Let's get to it."

They made their way into the passage between rooms. The hallway was still strewn with debris from windblown dust and leaves blown in from the windows at the end of the corridor. Elaine walked to the windows, passing a group of gentle servants moving in the opposite direction. Evidently, none of them wanted the windows closed. Elaine sat down on the sill at the end of the hall.

Melissa sat beside her. Together they gazed into the yard, eyes on the flock of blackbirds flying among the trees in the yard. There was no one there to talk to them, but given what Elaine had just told her, Melissa doubted the young witch wanted to get any closer to the demon.

"So that's a demon," said Melissa.

"That's Calferis."

"Do many demons transform into animals?"

"As far as I know," Elaine said, "he's always been an animal. He doesn't have another form."

"Or, you've never seen it," Melissa said.

"That's possible," said Elaine. "However, I did read a book on my family tree which said Calferis was given to us as a gift from above."

Melissa laughed. "I read a book about demons from Obnilen, and it mentioned each of them could take the form of a swarm of animals."

"Perhaps that describes Calferis." Elaine turned to Melissa. "Do you want to know how to get your essences to work for you?"

"Of course."

Elaine smiled. "I can help you, but first I need to know what you want to do."

Melissa spread her hands and then formed the shape of the spear out of the air, miming the haft to the blade. "I want to be able to use a weapon I've got skills with already."

Elaine shrugged her shoulders. "It's possible, if relatively simple."

"You say that, but how can I do it?"

"First of all, you need to know a different technique, one beyond matching if you want to train your sprites to perform an activity outside your body."

"And what technique is that?" Melissa asked.

"Bowing," said Elaine.

"As in showing respect to a ruler?"

Elaine nodded. "It is a simple technique, but one that many mages eschew in favor of more direct approaches. Normally, wizards are past the point of basic bowing. The technique allows one to submit to a demon or spiritual being."

Melissa raised her eyebrows. "Submit? I'd rather fight."

"I know," said Elaine, "but to fight the way you want, you'll need to submit to your own essences."

"I can submit to myself? All right."

"Your spirit consists of more than your sprites and banes. Many philosophers believe the two types of essence can be said to form the basis of the heart."

Melissa furrowed her brow. "Given that my essences are part of me, what can I do to submit to them?"

"I said many believe it, but it's far from literally true."

Melissa nodded, then frowned. "It's not true, then?"

"While it is common to think sprites and banes together form the human heart for those who know only simple magic, the human mind is separate from both forms of essences. Are you familiar with the concept of ego, or the inner self?"

Melissa raised her eyebrows. "The concept of a self within the self? That's philosophy, not magic."

Elaine patted the windowsill between them. "Some philosophy can be solid as stone."

"Can I use my inner self to address my essences?" asked Melissa.

"That's the basis of many more complex forms of magic. We must communicate with them as equals to use them as tools for purposes beyond ourselves. Once you can bow, you can send your sprites and banes from your body more easily, similar to the technique of separating Kadatz used to threaten you."

"I didn't know sprites and Banes could think and feel independent of their owners."

"I still don't know if they can, but they develop unhelpful attitudes when one approaches them from a position of superiority."

"Like me," said Melissa.

"A little," said Elaine. "With that demon outside, we need someplace else to practice. The basics of bowing can be taught anywhere. I learned them in a library."

Melissa glanced at Elaine. "You studied in a library because of the cold in the north?"

"I started lessons in midwinter," said Elaine, "and the books helped draw them out too. Sprites and banes are curious by nature. They can grant you many advantages, but you have to teach them your intentions by bowing."

"Then let's get started," said Melissa.

"You have some books," said Elaine, "but these lessons will be better served by one of the magic texts that my aunt keeps in her study."

"Do you think she'll allow that?" asked Melissa.

"Maybe not."

"She wants to teach us at her own pace," said Melissa.

"True." Elaine frowned, then climbed to her feet. "But, seeing as how we're friends, I'll get you one of those magic books, regardless."

Melissa felt her smile grow. "I guessed you preferred to read on the journey south over talking to people in the caravan."

Elaine laughed. "You did the same when not on watch. It's practical lessons I've got more trouble with."

Melissa ran a hand through her waves of hair, which fell back into place as her fingers passed. "We can't be that similar, can we?"

"I'd heard it said a person has the most trouble dealing with what they are themselves."

"What's that supposed to mean?"

"It means we don't like ourselves as much as we think we do, said Elaine.

"That actually makes sense to me."

Elaine's eyes brightened. "You and just about nobody else," she said. "It's thought of as an absurd aphorism, at least in the north."

"Well, Elaine," said Melissa.

"Well, Melissa," said Elaine.

Melissa grinned. "Let's find that book."

CHAPTER 17

SABEN

Saben and Rond returned a wounded Jaswei and the relic bell to the city. Jaswei slept on the way in the wagon most of the journey back, but she recovered somewhat by the time they reached the city. Soucot's north side looked far different on the road by light, then by the dark of the storm. The city came to life within its high walls and the glow of red and green in the outer orchards. Streets stank of filth and roared with the voices of vendors, a stunning assault on the senses after the countryside.

Saben helped Jaswei from the wagon and guided her upstairs to her room. Once she lay down, he left to take the bell to Eric. Rond waited behind in case Jaswei needed assistance.

Alone and feeling less for it, Saben approached the mercenary tavern. He entered through the small door in the alleyway, and let the short red-haired man lead him to the main room. The little man left him at the inner door. Saben approached the bar.

I'm all alone, he thought, *ever since my village was destroyed. Those demons will pay.* He nodded to Eric.

Eric put down the glass he'd been polishing. "Do you have it?"

"No one else managed to get it." Saben held out the bell and then placed it on the bar.

Eric whistled. "No one else came close."

"No one." Saben smiled.

Eric nodded. He swept the bell off the table. "I'll send the goods to the client."

"Good."

Eric glanced at Saben. "What happened to the other two?"

"They're both alive if that's what you're curious about," said Saben.

"It was a dangerous task."

"Indeed."

"You're more talkative than before," said Eric. "Anything else happen?"

"I need my pay," said Saben.

Eric shrugged and then slid a bag of clinking coins across the table. "That should cover it."

Saben inspected the bag. He counted thirty pieces of gold, enough to get the team through a whole month in the city. "I'll return soon." Saben left the mercenary tavern much heavier of pocket and lighter of heart.

* * *

He returned to the inn where the team was staying and went upstairs to join them in Jaswei's room. Rond let him inside before closing the door. Saben clapped the minstrel on the shoulder. "Thanks for looking after her." He nodded to Jaswei.

"She won't need my help much longer," said Rond. "She's healing rapidly."

Jaswei sat up in bed, she grinned at them both. "You know, I can understand you both."

"You heal fast," said Rond.

""I do everything quickly, including healing." She looked at the bandages on her arms. "These are unsightly. I'm glad I won't need them much longer."

Saben never saw Jaswei stay hurt for a long, even with wounds as severe as the ones she suffered from mausoleum guardians. They made a good team. Unlike what most assumed, he was the striker, and she was the shield to resist damage. They both could perform either role to some capacity, but she excelled at fast recovery.

"I'm going to my room."

Jaswei frowned at Saben. "Already?"

He shrugged.

Jaswei's face turned red. "I don't mind." She folded her arms. "Don't worry about it."

In his room alone, Saben sat before the Azel scroll they'd stolen from the library. He studied the inlays on the surface of the scroll's case, recognizing patterns and symbols from many different traditions along its length, but the scroll must wait for now. He needed a place to learn to master it, where he could safely call such power as contained within the demon's form while practicing.

Saben mustn't fall prey to the lack of caution that led so many others to disaster. He would have his revenge in time. The scroll before him assured that.

He picked up the sealed case and returned to the hallway outside, worried that while he carried the scroll others might recognize it. Moving quickly, he knocked on Jaswei's door again. Rond opened it fast.

"You're back."

Saben shrugged and then shouldered his way past Rond. Jaswei sat up as he entered. *Has some new feeling awakened in her?* Perhaps saving her life had changed things between them. He hoped not, because she seemed a good ally but a poor romantic partner.

Jaswei looked at the scroll in his hand. "You brought it here?"

Saben walked to the bed. "I thought you might want to see what we all endangered ourselves to get."

"Saben," Jaswei said, "you plan to use it now?"

"No," said Saben, "I want to study it. I need assistance for that."

"That's wise," said Jaswei.

"If I don't use the scroll," Saben said, "I don't know if I'll ever be strong enough."

"Strong enough for what?" asked Rond.

Jaswei and Saben exchanged glances. He nodded to her. "Strong enough to defeat an army of demons."

"An army?" Rond asked.

"A band of beings from above the world."

Jaswei frowned. "You still want revenge."

"As much as you want your old court clothes." Saben gestured to the cabinet and luggage cases containing Jaswei's wardrobe.

She frowned at him. Her eyes gleamed and her cheeks were bright with color. "I'll help you understand as much as I can, though I'm no master wizard."

"Neither am I, but I'll do the same," said Rond.

Rond and Jaswei both looked at Saben. He set the scroll case on the trunk at the foot of Jaswei's bed.

"We should find somewhere to decipher the text. Perhaps leaving the city would be best."

"Yeah," said Jaswei. "You're right."

A loud clatter of movement came from the window. Saben glanced out the pane and glimpsed a crowd in the street. The clear day allowed him a view of the angry faces of people who he'd seen in the street around the inn before.

"Somethings wrong," Saben said.

Jaswei lurched forward, then tried to stand. Saben took a step toward her as she put her feet to the floor, testing them. Another loud commotion reached the room, this time from above.

"Someone's on the roof," said Rond.

"Who would suddenly appear on a rooftop?" asked Jaswei.

Saben scowled as he remembered the flying man landing in the street in front of him a few days ago. "I would expect an immortal man."

"You mean that man we saw the other day?"

"Likely," said Saben.

Rond quaked where he stood. "Deckard, Hadrian? I heard he was in the city, but why would he be after us?"

Saben and Jaswei both turned toward Rond. "Who is Deckard Hadrian?" asked Saben.

"He's a demon Hunter, the greatest of them all, and he is immortal."

"Immortal?" said Jaswei, "I can't have heard that right."

"Those women I helped the other day talked about him. He is a servant of the one who rules Tancuon."

"The ruler of Tancuon?" Jaswei asked. "I thought the land was divided among countries."

"It is," said Rond, "but Mother Mercy unites everyone on the continent."

Saben grunted. "We must hurry."

He and Rond each took one of Jaswei's arms and helped her toward the door. Sounds on the stairs outside the hall approached them. Someone climbed the steps in a rush of steps. Whoever charged up the stairs might be as tall as Saben, judging by the sound and more quickly followed after that. *Hadrian brought reinforcements.*

A team of guards, Saben thought. *Can we escape so many?*

"They must be looking for the scroll," said Rond.

Saben tucked the case under one arm. He threw the door open and stormed across the hall for his sword and gear. "Help Jaswei get moving," he rumbled at Rond.

Men appeared at the end of the hallway as he emerged from his room. He gripped his sword in both hands, the empty baldric bound on his back and his new bag of coins clinking at his belt.

At the head of the soldiers, a thickly built man stood, but it was not Deckard Hadrian. The man wore the mantle of the Magister's Guild, complete with an emblem of the scroll and trident. The magister clapped his hands together. Saben felt the whole building creak around them.

Someone shouted from below. "Don't destroy my inn, damn it!"

The guards behind the mage exchanged nervous looks. "Sir," their leader said.

The mage stepped toward Saben. His fingertips flickered with electricity. "What we have here is a pack of thieves."

Jaswei and Rond emerged from the room into the hallway behind Saben. He faced the mage down the glinting length of his sword. The guards behind the mage shifted uneasily, their fears palpable enough to cut.

"Fall back," said the guard leader. "We're no use here. Surround the building."

Jaswei reached for the sheath of her sword, preparing to draw sprites from it, despite her wounds. The blade hissed but did not reform. When she was healing, Jaswei found magic difficult.

"Go the other way." Saben growled. His low voice a din like thunder down the hall. The guards scurried toward the stairs.

Lightning still flickering on the mage's fingertips formed a cage of electrical flares. A bolt of essence-directed energy shot down the hallway. Saben channeled the lighting bolt into his sword, pulling the shock into his essences that already reinforced the blade. Harmless light played on the weapon's edge.

Jaswei and Rond made for the opposite end of the building. They might be able to jump from a window onto the street if they hurried, but would have difficulty getting much further through the crowd and the guards.

Saben glowered at the mage before him. He raised his sword, but the roof was too low to swing it well. He backed away, lowering the blade. The mage grinned savagely.

He started forward, pursuing Saben and the others, no doubt buying time for the guards downstairs to spread out and surround the building. The situation worsened, even apart from the man on the roof they'd not yet seen.

As if in answer to his thoughts, a shadow passed across the window at the end of the hall. An instant later the windowpane exploded. Deckard Hadrian landed in a crouch at the end of the passage. His iron robe flowed around him as he rose to his full height. The rush of wind from outside scattered shards of broken glass upon the floor.

The guild mage laughed. "Now you're finished."

Saben gritted his teeth. "Not yet. But you're out of luck." He inhaled fast and then shouted.

The mage worked a counterspell with his hands, using his sprites to drain force from Saben's cry. The shock wave from Saben's throat did not rely on essences alone, driven by pure rage. He channeled his fury towards the demons into every decibel sound.

The sonic wave struck the mage and he collapsed to his knees, clutching his ears as the shock wave roared around him. Saben glared at the stricken man, then stepped forward, marching toward the stairs. Jaswei turned from the window.

Deckard Hadrian jumped into the air, arrowing toward Rond and Jaswei as they retreated toward Saben. Jaswei raised her sheath to block but no strike fell. Deckard landed between Saben and Jaswei and Rond.

The immortal raised a dark eyebrow. "Mercenaries, are you?"

Saben growled again, preparing another shout. Jaswei and Rond were on the other side of Hadrian. If he attacked the immortal, he would hit them both. If they could escape after that, he might have tried it, but they'd be in no condition to flee after enduring the blast of his voice.

He turned and faced Deckard Hadrian. Deckard took a fighting stance, right hand by his jaw.

"Are you going to try and punch me?" asked Saben, "No blade?"

"I don't need one." Deckard's other hand hung loosely at his side, nowhere near forming a fist.

"You know your arm. I know my sword," said Saben.

"I'm not afraid of you, boy."

"You think I'd fear some old man hurting me?" Saben released a laugh. The sound shook the whole building. Jaswei and Rond covered their ears. Deckard leapt backward, landing just outside the range of the cursed chuckle Saben had unleashed.

Deckard smiled. Saben glared at him.

"A fight is what you want, is it?" said Deckard.

"Not with you," said Saben. *Not with you, not at all.*

"You should give up that scroll," Deckard said. "I'll work out something with the governor's justice to help you."

"I doubt you'll do much," said Saben. "After I chop off your arm."

"Would you try to maim me?" Deckard said. "Mercenary?"

"Not if you stand aside."

Deckard squared his stance once more. Rond and Jaswei backed toward the window behind them and the immortal. The other hand still hung by Deckard's side.

What is he doing?

Saben charged at Deckard. He thrust his sword in front of him, making Deckard sidestep. Saben hurtled past, then felt pressure around his legs. Ties of light encircled his ankles. He fell to the floor, the boards rattling under his weight. He rolled onto his back, narrowly avoiding a downward strike from Deckard's fist. The board where his head had been split apart and fell away with a clatter.

Saben stared at the man as he snapped the bonds of sprite strings from his legs using the edge of his blade.

He moved to stand up, but Deckard's fingers wove more sprite strings about him from every angle. Jaswei struck in an instant. Her shoulder rammed into Deckard, making him stumble backward. She kept pushing him, and he moved slower, appearing fatigued. Her presence disrupted his sprites. She grabbed for his throat.

Though she was excellent with blades, but lacked the strength to throttle a man with one hand while he fought back.

Deckard shook her off. His face became a glowering visage, older and more twisted than before. He did not strike at Jaswei but retreated along the passage a few paces. His strings trailed behind him as he drew their magic into his fingers.

"So you aren't just a feather mage," said Saben. "You do more than fly."

Deckard hissed, his features contorted and unnaturally elongated. Though it could've been just a trick of the light, Saben thought he saw something off about the man in his build, a ripple of grayish veins climbed Deckard's face.

"Could he be using a demon form?"

Rond shook his head. "He doesn't have one of those,"

"How do you know that?" Jaswei hissed.

"I sang ballads about him," said Ron.

"A minstrel?" said Deckard. "Your singing days may be behind you." He rushed at Saben, darting to avoid Jaswei. She hurled her shoulder into his iron robe, then recoiled, bouncing off like a spear striking heavy armor. She hit the wall and sank to her knees.

Rond sprinted toward the window, far faster than he looked. Saben rushed to help Jaswei. Deckard struck with both fists at once. The force of the impact threw Saben backward and his feet left the floor. He flew out the window, taking Rond into the street with him.

Deckard didn't follow them. But settled on the edge of the window. His control over his flight was near-perfect.

Saben and Rond drifted slowly toward the street. Saben landed among a cluster of guards outside the inn, throwing dust and dirt into the air. Rond settled gently beside him. Hadrian had spared a sprite to slow his fall and save the two of them.

No longer hindered by the weakness of the building, Saben shouted out loud. His bellow flattened the guards with pure sonic rage. Saben tossed a stunned Rond across his shoulders and then ran toward the docks, not even grimacing under the weight. He hated that he'd left Jaswei behind, but he saw no way to rescue her at the moment. Deckard did not give chase.

Saben didn't recover his senses until they made it several blocks away, running at top speed. Survival was part of life. Until he could have his revenge, he had to keep running. Still, leaving Jaswei behind formed a pit in his stomach. His family would reproach him from their graves if they knew his cowardice.

He limped toward a ramshackle hovel by the water, still carrying the minstrel on his back. Rond had pointed out the shack to them earlier, but Jaswei preferred not to stay there. Saben had agreed with her the time. Things just changed.

CHAPTER 18

MELISSA

Melissa and Elaine sneaked into Lady Nasibron's study while the elder witch was absent. They crept through the dim light, from the steely windows. Motes of dust danced in the air between full bookshelves. The desk at the center of the room was covered in pages of parchment and unfurled scrolls. Elaine found a text suited for teaching the technique of bowing and they left the room as quickly and quietly as they'd entered.

Day turned to night, and as she and Elaine practiced, Melissa sensed her essence songs more keenly.

Later, she dug into the oddities of the book. Her sprite songs sounded louder and louder. The banes were subtler to her ears but still became audible as she read the notes on what to listen for in each type of song.

She made her way to the back of the book throughout the night, reading by candlelight. In the morning, she was exhausted. She had difficulty deciphering all the text, but she'd miss the book. Elaine returned the text to the study early the next day.

Teamwork. Lovely.

At practice that day, Melissa found she still heard all her essences far clearer than before. She began to draw them out little by little until they reached the surface of her skin. She was able to follow their movements and even made one of them dance on her fingertips.

There were only three, two sprites and one bane. She moved them around but couldn't yet make them do anything else. Other students seemed to be getting a hold of things faster. Now that she could hear them and understood how to show them respect, sprites and banes became more tools for Melissa, rather than obstacles. *Rusty tools though.* They did not yet obey, unshakable as metal.

Lady Nasibon approached her halfway through the day. "Having difficulties?"

"I can't seem to make them obey me."

"They're not going to obey you, because they're each part of you."

"Are you certain?" Melissa said.

Lady Nasibron raised her eyebrows. "Of course I am. I have studied essences my entire life. They react to what is inside us in our minds. Their essence might as well be our spirits. We must be careful not to influence them unduly."

Melissa focused on her sprites and banes, sweating as the day grew hot. Many other students, especially those in the mage guard rather than the governor's hand, went to find shade. They were all allowed to take breaks, but Melissa still needed to make more progress to satisfy herself. She wanted to see her sprites and banes do something useful, anything to demonstrate her worth to the governor and her teacher.

The number of other students training gradually diminished. Niu and Tal retreated to the shade to rest. Eventually, even the stubborn Kelt Crayta retired to the shadows of the wall as well.

Only Melissa and one other student remained on the field. Suya Nattan, the governor's sword servant, stood focusing her sprites and banes into her blade, the sword she carried for herself. The governor's blade remained strapped to her belt in its sheath.

Suya was a lithe and flexible individual, but her sprites seemed less willing to react than most of the other students. *Like me,* Melissa thought. Prior training seemed to increase the difficulty in learning magic rather than diminish it. Melissa and the others all carried tension in their practice. The students watching from the shade, gazed at them, in almost-reverent silence.

Let them stare, Melissa said to herself. She had to continue pushing, or she would never accomplish her goals. She should have learned the basics of magic years ago. When the magisters drove her out of the city, she'd been forced to leave magic behind. *No more delays,* she told herself.

Melissa sent a sprite darting from her fingertips, tipped by her iron bane. She sent both of them down the length of her spear, squinting down the weapon's length. The separated sprite sang through the air along the haft of her spear, making the air ripple with its movement. The iron bane hurtled forward, passing the end of the long weapon, and then struck the earth. Melissa's eyes widened as the bane dove into the soil at high speed, leaving a scar across the yard, burning with steam. The bane tore a black line of dirt through both grass and earth.

Suya spun and stared at Melissa, shock on her face. "How did you do that?"

Melissa wiped the sweat from her brow. "I don't know," she said. "I got frustrated. I really don't know."

Suya shook her head, her eyes wide. "You'd better find out," she said. "You need to do that again!"

Melissa reeled, staggering under the burden of her fatigue and disorientation. She sank onto the grass in a sitting position. The essences Melissa had released returned to her and their return steadied her. Separating sprites and banes for yourself was a dangerous prospect for one's consciousness but the damage done to the yard was considerable for one essence. *I could use more of those. If I have more essences, I'll make a much better wizard, won't I?*

Melissa and the others broke from training just before dinner as the sun began to set.

Within the feasting hall, the long tables stood against the walls, and most of the chairs were put away. The student mages ate and drank at four clusters near the center of the room. At one of the small tables sat the hand of the governor. The five of them assembled as a group for the first time since the governor chose them.

Suya sat across the table from Melissa with Niu on Melissa's right. Hilos settled in on her left. Kelt Crayta sagged in a chair next to Suya on the other side of the table. The five of them occupied a higher status than the other soldiers and mages, but everyone had worked hard today. The five of them would become the most senior members of the new order of the governor's mage guard.

Elaine approached their table. Melissa turned and greeted her. She waved a hand at a spare chair nearby, on Niu's other side. Elaine took the seat and pulled a plate toward her. Melissa smiled. The local fish and scallops at their table tasted delicious. Melissa wondered if Elaine had seen them training earlier that day. She had been suspiciously absent from the yard. However, much of the palace had a view of where the mages practiced.

"Good job using your bane today," said Elaine. "I saw that blast from a window."

Melissa chuckled. "Do you think I can repeat using a bane like that to attack?"

"I suppose you could," said Elaine.

"It's better than nothing. I was recruited as a war mage."

Niu raised her eyebrows. "It looked pretty strong to me."

Suya chewed thoughtfully, eyelids low with a pensive expression.

Hilos folded his hands and put his plate aside. He nodded to Elaine. "You, my lady, are quite perceptive of the needs of the students. Perhaps you will be a good teacher yourself one day."

"You are already," said Melissa.

Niu laughed. "Weren't you at each other's throats yesterday?"

"We worked some things out. "Melissa smiled.

Elaine laughed. "You could say that again."

Melissa glanced at Kelt. "Did you make any progress on your techniques?"

Kelt nodded. "Not as much as yours."

"You've got a better concept for yours, though."

"I think whatever you did today is what I'm trying to do," he said.

"Agreed," said Suya.

Niu glanced at Melissa. "I think if we could all shoot that kind of attack, we might be of real use to the governor in a battle."

"There's more to battles than shooting things," said Melissa. "But I see your point."

"Real mages don't have to do battle with magic arrows," said Elaine. "There are subtler weapons than spears. Those are all blunt instruments, metaphorically. Mages need to use power more thoughtfully to be truly a match for experienced opponents."

"You mean…" Melissa started.

"I mean, we need to get creative with our magic. I don't think my aunt will give you more sprites and banes to work with if you don't demonstrate creativity."

"Creativity?" Tal asked, as the only member of the mage guard sitting at this table, thanks to his sister.

"Yes," said Elaine. "Creativity is one of the most important aspects of becoming a mage. If you can't think a new idea into being, you can't send your essences to execute on that plan. Our practice is important, but originality can make your opponents thrown off, as my aunt says."

"I suppose we should be training our minds as much as our sprites and banes," Melissa said.

Elaine nodded. "If you don't, you could quickly fall behind again."

Suya nodded, finally finishing her food. She put down her fork. "I think a sword is unnecessary for someone who already knows how to use one. We should be training our magic to do things our weapons can't."

"Last I checked," said Melissa, "my spear can't cut through the earth like that."

"Fair point," said Suya. "Though the governor may want us to do more than simply smash things."

"What does creativity mean for each of us?" asked Niu. "Should we all be learning to fly like Deckard Hadrian?"

"Deckard is a special case," said Elaine. "Very few mages can emulate feathers the way he does. I think it's possible others could do it, but I've never heard of anyone else who managed to learn that kind of magic in our current age."

"I've read about Prince Geldingstar, and he was supposedly a feather mage. The book I studied last night mentioned him."

Niu glanced at her. "You got a new book?"

Melissa flushed, unable to think of a cover for the theft. "Elaine lent me a book." She lowered her voice. "We, uh, borrowed it from Lady Nasibron."

Niu glanced at Elaine, who shrugged. "I took a volumed from my aunt's study. It's back now, so no need to tell her about it."

"You helped Melissa," said Niu. "Can't you help the rest of us too?"

Elaine nodded. "I should have thought sooner. I can tutor each of you and we can help you become better mages, maybe even wizards, faster than my aunt can on her own. Besides, I need more practice myself." Elaine glanced at Melissa with a grin. She returned the expression.

CHAPTER 19

DECKARD

It wasn't often one saw a mural in a dungeon. Nevertheless, by the yellow light filtering through the barred windows with their iron shutters open, Deckard Hadrian traced the unpleasant image on the wall opposite the cells.

Red and yellow paint, peeling with the ravages of time, portrayed the demise of the Kanori fleet on the far side of the bay from Soucot. A victory for the forces of Tancuon meant spilling the blood of countless sailors and soldiers in the surf. Deckard remembered the battle well. His apprentice at the time had destroyed one of the Kanori fortress ships with a blast of wind and fire that set the neighboring vessels, one from each side, ablaze. The red and orange at the top of the mural depicted those flames in fading shades of infernal color.

Eighteen years had passed since he had been to that place, though Deckard could cross the Bay of Charin under less peril from pirates and the strange wiles of the fishers than most. If he flew high enough, he could pretend he didn't feel the presence of the other entities dwelling beneath the dark waves.

A curse on this place for reminding me of you, he thought, as he swept down the passage. How many of Kanor's warrior and leadership class had shriveled away in the cells of this palace? *How many rot here still, in body or in mind?*

After the terrible battle, Deckard wondered, but he did not care to find the answer. Too many lives of those he'd loved had been lost that day. No, the dungeon and it's prosaic inhabitants were not part of his mission any more. Deckard left the horrid mural behind as he descended a flight of steps to one of the dungeon's lower levels.

His eyes adjusted to the darker passage, lit only by cold blue-white bane lights in sconces on the wall every few yards. The air was damp, and a chill crept into his feet through the soles of his boots. The cells along this passage were occupied. Having spent time in his share of cells colder than these, Deckard kept himself from looking at their occupants. He could become too sympathetic to the plight of prisoners, and for now, his destination lay yet further below.

Someone spoke up ahead. A moment later, an answering voice reached his ears. The first voice belonged to an older man, the second voice was younger judging by the speed and sense of verve, and belonged to a woman.

"I don't care where you put her as long as it has magical locks and bars," said the woman. "I know we're short on that kind of cell, but she requires it."

"I understand, Lady Nattan, but—"

"It's not my whim. The governor and Lady Nasibron insist."

"Understood. I will clear one of the lesser offenders and request an additional detail for him. As for her..."

Deckard rounded the corner at the end of the passage. He found Governor Lokoth's sword servant with her hands clapped on the arms of a second woman, the one Deckard had caught in the city and then turned over to the guards. The foreign prisoner's hands were bound together from wrist to wrist. Her thick, yellowish hair was pushed up and back in a Najean knot. The magical bindings, Deckard recognized, could keep most magic users from drawing their commands and symbols in the air. He counted himself lucky for the number of times one of his captors thought that meant he was powerless. Most of those captors slept beneath the earth by now, whether they were mortal or demon.

The palace interrogator, a weary older knight of the Imperial Order of Mercy, turned toward Deckard. "Lord Hadrian, I was not told to expect you would follow up with the prisoner." He bowed his head.

The sword servant, Suya Nattan, bowed as well. Deckard judged by her dark hair and pale, dominion features, similar to his own that she was also a northern transplant to Lowenrane. With Tandace Lokoth's household hailing from the Geteren Well Country, that made sense.

"Rest easy, both of you," he said. "I've not been fully informed, so please talk."

"You know of the theft at the library in the city," said Suya. "A few vagabonds made off with scrolls, including this woman."

Deckard nodded. "I apprehended her myself but found no magic scrolls."

Suya pushed the yellow-haired woman forward with pressure on her arms. "The two men escaped."

"You still haven't found them?" Deckard asked.

"No. And they must still have their stolen scrolls with them." Suya shook her head. "Forgive me, I don't know anything more."

"I will find out the rest," said the interrogator. "Do you wish to assist me, Lord Hadrian?"

"I'm not a torturer," said Deckard. "However, ask me before you do any permanent damage. Mind her tongue and face. Too many of your profession make mistakes that render answering impossible."

"With respect, I can do my job, Lord Hadrian."

"I have no doubt. Now, please excuse me." He made his way around the three in the passage and then continued toward the staircase, going deeper into the dungeon.

"My lord," asked the interrogator, following him a few paces. "Excuse me, but where are you going?"

"I have other business below," said Deckard.

"May I ask—"

"You may not. Go to your task, sir knight." Deckard turned, moving his iron robe about his shoulders. He left the interrogator behind, then continued down the stairs. The knight did not follow or protest further.

Another few passages and another few stairways later, he reached the lowest point of the dungeon, five levels beneath the ground. At a dead-end in the hallway, across from an unlocked and vacant cell, he remembered the patterns in the rough stone barrier. This was the place. Beneath him lay the mightiest world well in all of Lowenrane. He tapped the tiles with his shoes, trying to find the proper sequence. After a few minutes of his odd dance, he hit the correct points in sequence.

In the vacant cell nearby, the wall shifted with the grinding sound of stone on stone. A path opened, revealing a rough-hewn stone passage leading down to the original cavern the palace had been built upon. The mix of pale and vivid light from free-flying essences gave him enough visibility to follow the tunnel to a place where it widened.

Mystic lights flitted and glided over the abyssal pit of shaped demon stone. Its walls ended at the very edge of the earth, so the whole room seemed drawn to its near-infinite darkness within the world well of Lowenrane.

"Long time," Deckard whispered. He approached the edge of the well, then glanced over it at the inky dark drop.

Deckard Hadrian could fly the world over but still feared to fall in a place like this one. He stepped away. Circling the pit, he sniffed the air. The place was a bit damp, but he neither heard nor saw nor smelled any sign of a demon clambering up from the well. Rogue monstrosities must remain below, said the law of Mother Mercy. She would brook no evil-doers to walk the surface. *No evil-doers not sanctioned by her rules at least*, Deckard added mentally.

"You were intent on finding this place," said Tandace Lokoth from the entrance behind him.

His gaze drifted to her. "Governor, I am a demon hunter first."

"I am not surprised. I know you have your many missions, and we mortals are rarely privy to them all, even those of us chosen by mercy to sit a throne."

"Wise," said Deckard. "Though you're lucky I was not tasked with maintaining this place's secrecy."

"You wouldn't kill an imperial governor of mercy."

I have tried before, he thought absently. "Yes," he said.

She nodded. "I trust you see all is as it should be?"

"Indeed. I trust you a have told no one of this place unless necessary?"

"You can trust me, yes." Tandace Lokoth smiled in the light of the dancing spirit motes. "Perhaps we should return to the surface together, my lord."

"As you say." He followed her out of the cavern, then through the dungeon to the palace above. At the surface, he moved to part from her side.

"Where are you going?" she asked.

"I have questions that need answering in a different city."

"Leaving so soon after all the trouble I took to summon you here?"

"I'll return o Soucot before dawn," he said, nodding out the gates to the long arc of the rings cutting through the sky to circumscribe the world's edge.

"Can you fly to the city and return in such little time?" Tandace frowned.

He chuckled. "You studied witchery, so you ought to know. There are other ways one can reach that place."

The governor nodded. "Be at court tomorrow, Lord Hadrian."

"As you say."

He swept out the open gate of the palace, and then descended the slope of the citadel into Soucot. Deckard made his way to one of the shrines that ringed the citadel's walls at hundred-yard intervals. Passersby would say they saw the lord of winds stop before the miniature temple, bordered by its two arched blades. He bowed before a circular altar on the pedestal between them. The passersby would say he vanished in the blink of an eye.

ELAINE

Elaine tried to relax the next day, taking some time to herself before beginning tutoring the hand of the governor personally. She went into the city, looking for supplies to help them improve their understanding of essences. The five of them were fine material, but unforged at this moment. They could be useless in the end, or utterly overpowering if she and Lady Nasibron trained them well.

She took a winding route through the streets that brought her close to the docks. On her way, she passed the library and spotted fewer guards around it than before. She went inside quickly to ask if the stolen demon scroll had been found. The librarian told her otherwise, but that the watch had captured one of the thieves.

"One of the thieves?" Elaine asked.

The librarian stifled a laugh, then said, "It was a woman who came to Tancuon from across the bay. There were two others with her, a big man with a sword and a fat thief who also plays at being a minstrel in the city."

"A minstrel?"

"Quite so. We have the names, so in time they'll be caught. Serves them all right for stealing from the library."

"I suppose it does," said Elaine. "What were their names?"

"The big man was called Saben, and the woman who they captured is said to be from Naje. I can't say her name right. The minstrel is a local named Rond, but he's also a ne'er-do-well by all reports."

"Saben." Elaine frowned. "I met him."

The librarian shrugged her shoulders. "Perhaps you did, but if you did, you no doubt were lucky to get away without a scratch. He seems a vicious brute. The guards had real trouble trying to trap him because he wields some kind of magic."

Elaine nodded as numbing dread crept into her mind. Saben seemed a reasonable person when she first met him. Quiet, when he talked to others, he seemed normal when he spoke with her. Elaine went on her way. She approached the docks and acquired a handcart with a list of supplies she gathered before returning to the palace.

CHAPTER 20

SABEN

The city looked bleak to Saben from his hiding place by the docks. He waited with Rond for a few days, taking his time to recover some of the bruises and cuts acquired in the fall. Despite Hadrian setting Rond down carefully, both of them had still flown through a broken window. The battering by Hadrian, only underscored how weak Saben still knew himself to be.

Saben and Rond stayed in the shack by the dockside. The area swarmed with activity every day, but no one thought to look in their ruined old hovel. Despite their safety relative to moving around outside, Saben quickly grew irritated with only leaving at night to scrounge for food. He wasn't getting any stronger like this.

Rond, on the other hand, seemed in his element, despite having lost most of his supplies in their flight from the inn. He still had a lute and his voice, much to Saben's annoyance. He talked. Too much.

Rond and Saben sat through the days, gradually smelling worse in the sweltering heat.

On the sixth day, Saben had enough and set out into the street in broad daylight, despite Rond's protests. The moment he emerged from the hovel into the alleyway beside it, he turned and saw a skinny local man watching him. The man wore spectacles, a necessity for some Tancuonese near-completely unseen in the east.

The man approached with a swagger in his step, and nodded to Saben. "I was wondering when you'd come out of there."

"Who are you?" asked Saben.

"My name is Deel. I'm looking for someone with a useful set of skills."

"Skills? Like mine?"

"Mercenaries with real magic are uncommon. You've got some potential, you know."

"Men like me aren't easy to find anywhere."

Deel adjusted his glasses. "It's the management of the nations and settlements of the whole land."

"Are you from Tancuon?" asked Saben.

"I am. Though further to the north." He smiled.

"What do you want?"

"I have a job for you."

"What kind of job?"

"I'll show you. No need for the minstrel to join us. He won't be of much use."

"I didn't say I was taking your job."

Deel shrugged. "I suppose I should offer your payment first?" He grinned and drew a shimmering shape from the pocket of his coat.

He held the object for Saben to lean close to see. It was one of Jaswei's hairpins.

"Where did you get that?"

"I'm able to go wherever I wish," said Deel.

"Including the palace?"

"Including the palace dungeons," said Deel. "And if you help my friends and me, we can free your friend from that very place."

"I owe her much."

Deel's grin widened. "Then come with me."

Saben nodded.

They made their way to the docks. The vessel tethered to the pier looked barely afloat, with a leaking hull, tattered sails, and a broken mast. No doubt, it had not moved in some time. The anchor looked steady enough to be dug in at the bottom of the harbor, probably deep enough the chain would break before it could be hauled to the surface.

"This is my houseboat," said Deel. "Borrowed, of course."

Saben frowned. "Not much more than a wreck."

"From what I understand, you've traveled on vessels in more scanty repair than her."

"Are we going somewhere?" asked Saben. "I don't want to sink anything just by stepping on board."

"Have confidence."

"I'll have patience. For now."

"Fine. Now follow me. This is where my friends are waiting."

They boarded the leaky ship.

DECKARD

Deckard entered the maladrite city and swept through the streets, moving toward the House of Mercy.

Mother Mercy, who held the world in awe. Mother Mercy, who ruled Tancuon with a fist of iron and silk. Mother Mercy, who governed without governing. Mother Mercy, who must not be disrespected. She gave him his power and held him at his limitations. She commanded his movements over the many years, though he rarely spoke with her himself.

He marched through the streets, closing with the house. The house of mercy made for a towering edifice, much larger than any structure in the human world. Despite the grandeur of the city and the structures all around, Mother Mercy's golden palace sang a song of doom with its essences as Deckard approached. He stiffened is resolved.

Mother Mercy allowed many to enter the house. As one of her agents, Deckard could expect an easy entrance when he knocked on the door.

He slipped past creatures that appeared mostly human but which were far from mortal. He approached the outer gates. Maladrites of all kinds filled the streets, moving and talking with each other. They were quieter than human traffic, but some loomed far larger and cast more conspicuous shadows. Deckard raised his fist and knocked on the doors. The gates yawned open.

In time he returned to Soucot as the world grew dark with the coming of night.

MELISSA

Melissa worked with the sprites and banes inside her mind and heart. She struggled at first to make them do anything other than attack or resist. Melissa needed not to break them down, but to respect them enough to access the power and knowledge they contained. She knew too much and understood too little.

She and the other members of the governor's hand met within the palace walls. The hand occupied one side of the yard, while the rest of the mage guard trained on the other. Niu and Kelt formed one practice pair while Hilos went to practice his locks at the nearby tower door. Suya and Melissa began to talk out their plans with Elaine.

"I could use my swords as a focus for magic," said Suya. "Though I may not need another weapon like them."

"Tools can be useful to direct your essences," said Elaine.

Melissa frowned. "I bet I could use my spear in the same way."

"Sprites and banes you've taught to bow can attend any object you're touching with your senses." Elaine smiled at Suya. "Your weapons may have limitations, but they may also prove themselves useful tools."

"A sword is a weapon, not a tool," said Suya. "Though I can nearly see what you mean."

Elaine folded her arms. "You'll need to see more clearly if you want to continue serving with the rest of the governor's hand."

"I'm not a fool," said Suya. "I'm nervous."

"I understand," said Elaine.

Melissa glanced at where Kelt and Niu lined up to spar. "Likewise."

"You don't get it, though," said Suya. "I am the governor's sword servant. If I can't learn magic, I may lose my position."

"I could suffer the same fate, not having any other real talents," Melissa said.

"I suppose you're right." Suya sighed.

Elaine tapped her chin. "Do both of you need your weapons that much? Suya, what exactly brought you to this palace?"

"I'm not some veteran of countless battles. I'm not some knight. I'm not even a retainer of a noble family by heredity. I am from the north, but I barely became an apprentice with the sword in that region. Luckily, I excelled well enough by the time my parents brought me south that I could enter the tournament in Soucot. I joined the governor's service to prove my willpower and I've made it almost as high as one can go without becoming a noblewoman."

Suya scowled. "The problem is magic. If I can't hold my own with mages even by becoming one, I won't have a claim to my position any longer. One of the other members of the hand will probably be asked to take my place."

"Just because magic offers powerful advantages, that doesn't mean your sword skills are worthless," said Elaine.

"Elaine's right," said Melissa. "She and I talked about this, but spears and swords can be excellent for directing your sprites and banes once you've extended them from your body."

Suya shook her head. "That seems far off. Don't play games with me."

Elaine shrugged her shoulders. "You're not getting any closer by complaining."

"Fair enough." Suya folded her arms. "Where can I start, though?"

"Suya," said Melissa, "could we spar? I think better on my feet."

"A sword against a spear? Doesn't seem fair." Suya touched the hilt of her weapon. "How skilled are you with short blades?"

"Not very," said Melissa. "How are you with polearms?"

"I'm all right," said Suya. "Better with swords, though."

"Meet me halfway, then."

She turned to where Kelt and Niu fought back and forth. He swung his massive oar as if it was an ax on a long pole. Niu danced out of the way, waving her staff.